EMERSON WOLVES   BOOK 4

KATHI S. BARTON

This is a work of fiction. Names, characters, places, and incidents are products of the author's imagination or are used fictitiously and are not to be construed as real. Any resemblance to actual events, locations, organizations, or person, living or dead, is entirely coincidental.

World Castle Publishing, LLC
Pensacola, Florida
Copyright © Kathi S. Barton 2015
Hardback ISBN: 9781629893440
Print ISBN: 9781629893457
eBook ISBN: 9781629893464
First Edition World Castle Publishing, LLC, October 5, 2015
http://www.worldcastlepublishing.com

Cover: Karen Fuller
Editor: Eric Johnston
Editor: Maxine Bringenberg

Eight years ago

"Where are you, girl? Girl? Where the heck have you gotten yourself to now?" Dawn curled tighter into the hole she'd found for herself and tried to control her breathing. It would not do to get caught when she'd gotten so far this time. "Girl? You'd better darn well answer me. It's not gonna go well for you if you don't come out now."

She had no intentions of ever going back. Dawn knew that if she was caught this time, not only would she be beaten again, but she'd more than likely die. Or she'd try her best to die this time. She was too tired to keep doing this. When her uncle moved by where she was, Dawn curled tighter into her ball and stopped breathing. He stood not two feet from her, and she knew that he'd only have to turn just a little to find her.

As soon as he moved on she was tempted to bolt again, but that had been what got her caught before. He wasn't faster than her, but she was weighted down with the chains still on her ankles, and there wasn't any way for her to shift and outrun him either. Staying still, even with the need to run now beating at her, Dawn closed her eyes and tried to think of anything but him.

She had been seven when she was brought to her uncle and aunt—brother and sister-in-law to her mom—and at first it had been nice. Her mother had been in prison for about three months before they'd figured out she had a kid, and the authorities had come looking for her. Stealing food had made her feel horrible, but she had a plan to pay everything back. That hadn't worked out so well so far.

About a year after she'd started living with Uncle Basil and Aunt Neva, he'd supposedly lost his job. She never really understood what it was he'd done, but just one day she was sat at the table and told that she was no longer going to have the luxuries that she'd had before. Not that she could remember having any, but Aunt Neva took great pride in the fact that Dawn was going to lose them.

"And you'll work around here too. Cooking one meal a day for us, and we'll do the rest." Again, something that she'd been doing anyway. "There will no longer be a ride to school. You'll have to walk back and forth, and starting tomorrow, you'll pack your lunch. No more free lunches for you."

"But I do that already."

The slap had knocked her off the chair and into the stove behind her. As she lay there, stunned and hurting, Aunt Neva stood over her screaming at her to get up. Dawn did finally get up and sit back in the chair, only to be knocked back again, by her uncle this time. She didn't remember much of what happened that night after that. And it continued over the years, but mostly with her aunt giving out the hits and Uncle Basil just telling her what a disappointment she was, and how he wished he'd never said yes to taking her in.

For many years her routine had rarely changed. Dawn did the laundry, another job that had been added to her list when she'd been caught sitting at the table reading the newspaper that had been wrongly delivered to their house. While the laundry was washing or drying, she'd make their meals and then clean up after them. The living room had to be cleaned after they went to bed, but no vacuuming. Their bedroom was cleaned daily, the bed made, and the bathroom had to be spotless by ten or there would be hell to pay. While it wasn't the cleanest house in the world, it was all she'd really known. Dawn could recite every story they'd told her about her mom—every evil thing that they said she did—and what Dawn should and should not be doing to help them out, as they were so good to let her stay with them. Then she'd turned eighteen.

Her birthdays were never acknowledged. The day would only be noticed by her, and for the most part, she was fine with that. At any given time up until that point she could have told anyone the days, hours, and even the minutes remaining until that particular time in her life came to her. She was leaving them then. It was her right as an adult.

Her eighteenth birthday had started out just like any other Tuesday. She had gathered the wash up and was putting the first load in the machine when her belly began to churn. Not like she was hungry—she knew that feeling all too well—but like she was going to be sick. Going to the bathroom had produced nothing more than a bit of bile, but she didn't feel any better.

As the day wore on, she began to sweat. Her body felt strange, and she could swear that there was a monster inside of her...a monster that wanted out of her. By dinner she could hardly move, her muscles ached, and her skin felt as if it was going to peel away from her.

As the dinner simmered on the stove, Dawn had gone into the yard to get some fresh air. Screaming with the pain, she fell to her knees, and just as the consuming pain took her breath away, it was gone. She knew that something was wrong…so terribly wrong. Dawn fell twice trying to walk, and then realized that she was no longer Dawn, but something with fur and paws.

Dawn was able to move around after a few minutes, and had liked the way she felt. Her body was…she supposed it was stronger than her human body had been, and for some reason she'd not been scared or freaked out by the change. Just wonderfully happy. Then her uncle had come out of the house, and things went bad fast.

Her uncle stomping by her again brought her out of her thoughts. She didn't move, and for now that seemed to be working for her. He was getting madder by the second, and she nearly smiled at that. But him being pissed would only be harder on her if he caught her.

"Darn you, girl, when I find you, I'm going to whip you with a stick. Where the heck are you?" She saw him twice more as he moved by her hiding place. Her legs were cramping up and she had to pee, but those were minor things compared to what he'd do if he caught her again. "Girl, you are starting to really make me mad at you, and you know how it hurts you when I lose my temper."

Dawn stayed where she was until the moon was high in the sky. She'd not heard her uncle in a long time, but that didn't mean he wasn't out there somewhere just waiting for her to get up and show him where she was. But she had to move. It was that or be so sore she'd not be able to get away if he was gone.

Moving slowly to let the pins and needles move out of her muscles, Dawn picked up her bag of things and slowly moved her head above the hole where she'd been hiding.

Nothing. Lifting her nose to the air, she could smell him, but it was faint now. His scent was faded, long gone from where she was. Pulling the bag and her chain with her, she moved out of the hole. Still cautious, she moved from tree to tree, hardly making a sound as she did so. It was the most delicious feeling she'd ever had.

Walking with the moon in front of her, Dawn knew that she'd make it to a town soon. It had taken her four different failed escape attempts before she got to this point. And she had made better decisions on what to take with her too. Food was a necessity, but it was the compass she'd found one day when she'd been in the big shed, as well as all the money she'd been stashing away since her eighteenth birthday, that was going to be the most help. It had only been a few dollars here, some change there, that she'd found when doing the laundry. Lucky for her when she'd been caught all those times before, neither of them had found those two items.

It was dawn when she stopped. The town was ahead of her; she could see the glow of the city lights. But Dawn knew that going into the little burg would be a mistake. She had on clothing that was filthy, and there was a shackle on both her ankles. The long chain was attached to another one that was around her neck. It would be hard to hide and even harder to explain. Dawn was sure she looked like a prison escapee.

Instead of going to the town to beg for help, she made it to the big barn that was near the road. Spending the day there was preferable to anything that she might find in town. She hid in the top of it, where the sweet hay was the nicest bed she'd had in a long while, and fell asleep.

The voices woke her. A man and a boy were talking about the sheep that had been stolen. Dawn knew who had stolen them. Her uncle took great pride in his ability to turn a buck at someone else's expense. Listening to them talking, she knew what it was costing them to have so many of his herd taken.

"We'll have to cut corners, you know." The boy said yes, and Dawn wondered what sort of punishment he'd put on the little boy because of her uncle. "Maybe we'll only be able to get one popcorn instead of two when we go see that movie tonight."

"Oh, Dad. You don't even like popcorn anyway." The child and man laughed, and Dawn smiled at the sound of it. "Maybe we can use my savings to go tonight. I been saving and saving."

"No, that's your money, son. You're going to go to college with that, and can take care of your old dad when he's too senile to take care of himself." They laughed again and moved out of the barn. Dawn sat back, thinking about the conversation as she ate her banana.

She was now twenty years old and no one had talked to her like that since she'd been a child. Not in the whole nearly fourteen years she'd been with her aunt and uncle. Even then her mom would yell at her for hours about an A on her report card and not an A-plus, and no matter how many times she'd tried to explain to her that they didn't give that kind of grade, she expected her to have them.

Dawn knew now why she'd done it. Her mom had wanted her to have a better life than she had right then. Fat lot of good it had done either of them.

Lying back down, she decided that she'd stay one more night, then move on. There was no way she was going to get caught now. This was the furthest she'd ever gotten, and she was going to make the best of it somehow.

Dawn stayed for three days. The first night, after the house had darkened, she searched the barn for anything to remove the shackles from her body. She finally found a long screwdriver, but ended up stabbing it into her foot and not removing the chains at all. It had hurt like hell but she did a good job of cleaning it up, and by the morning of the fourth day of her freedom, she was ready to move on.

She hadn't gotten far when an expensive looking car nearly ran her down.

The lady had been really nice to her, talking to her calmly while Dawn had tried to clean most of the blood and dirt off her pants. These were her cleanest pair, and as she had no way of knowing when she'd be able to wash them, it frustrated her to no end that they were dirty. When the woman reached out and touched her fingers to her hand, Dawn felt a burn up her arm like she'd touched a hot burner.

"He'll find you tomorrow if you don't let me help you." Dawn fell back again, soaking her pants through as she stared at the woman. "My name is Addie Parker. I live up the road about three miles. But your uncle is going to find you tomorrow while you're in a restaurant asking about a job."

"I don't know what you're talking about." The woman nodded. "I'm just out taking a walk."

Her voice had been scratchy from lack of use, and she was sure the woman thought she was nuts. Then she knelt down to her level, uncaring of the mud and mire that was getting on her nice clothing, and put her hand on the shackles. She touched the one around her neck and finally spoke.

"He put this one on you when you first shifted. He said that it was the only way to keep you from killing them in their sleep. It was used to chain you to the wall in the bathroom." Dawn nodded at her, terrified beyond anything she'd ever been before. "These he put on you after he read that if you shifted while wearing them that you'd sever your feet. He's not a nice person, is he?"

"No. Neither is my aunt." The woman nodded. "How do you know these things? Is he...do you know him? Is he talking to you about me? I'm not going back there."

"No. You're not. But he's going to find you if you don't trust me." A car drove around them, and Addie shielded her from being seen by its occupants. Then Addie helped her into her car. She spoke as she drove, telling her about where she would be safe from now on. "I have a cottage on the property not far from where you lived before. It'll be safer for you there. No one knows about it but a few, and it's too close for him to think you'd go there. No one ever goes out there anymore. They used to use it for a hunting shed, but it's been a long time since anyone hunted on the property. I'd take you to my home, but I'm afraid he'd figure it out. Not that I'm afraid of him, but people will talk and he'll get to you."

"Why are you doing this?" Addie drove for a few minutes, and Dawn started to ask her again, but she finally answered.

"No one should be abused. And you seem like a nice person." She glanced at her. "You *are* a nice person. I want to help. And in turn, you can help me."

"I don't have anything to help you with. I don't have but a few dollars." Addie grinned and told her how much she had to the penny. "How do you know that?"

"I can read you...your mind and your body. You're very malnourished. The wound on your foot is healing, but you need to rest for a while. You've been beaten up a great deal, starved when you pissed them off, and you don't have nearly enough fluid in your body to keep you well." As they turned down an overgrown drive, Addie continued. "I need someone to keep an eye on the place. Keep strays, including people, out of the house. I can pay you, in money or food, but I'd suggest food for now so that you won't have to travel into town. There is still the chance that he'll find you."

"I'm not going back." Addie told her she didn't want her to either. "His name is Basil Combs. My aunt is Neva. He lost his job when I was eight, and they've not had much in the way of income since."

"How long ago was that?" Dawn told her it had been fourteen years, give or take a few months. "I'm so sorry you had to live like that. It's not right that anyone should live like an animal, the way they were treating you."

Dawn wanted to cry. She didn't, but she wanted to. When they pulled up in front of the little house, she wanted to beg Addie to let her stay there forever. As they moved to the house, Dawn held her chains to her, wondering if this was all a scam and her uncle was going to be in there waiting for her. Addie turned to her before she opened the door.

"No one is here. I swear to you, so long and you don't leave this area, he won't find you." Dawn nodded. "I'm going to let you in, then go to the barn. There should be something in there we can use to get these off you. Go ahead and look the place over, and we'll see what you need to keep you safe for a while."

The house was huge in comparison to the one she had lived in, with two bedrooms on the second floor and one on the bottom. The kitchen was outdated, but it had a big stove and oven and a nice refrigerator. There was a tall freezer in a sort of walk in room with no door, as well as a washer and dryer. It, too, was outdated and had a strange smell when she'd opened it, but it was nothing she couldn't clean up. Everything needed a good scrubbing, but Dawn was used to hard work.

When Addie came back in, she had some tools and what looked like a small saw. As Dawn was told to have a seat, Addie gave her some information about the house. "The linens are in a large plastic tote in each bedroom closet. I think there are some quilts there too, but I'm not sure. I'll bring you heavier blankets if you need them the next time I come here. There are cleaning supplies, I think, under the sink, as well as pots and pans. There are other things you might need in boxes in the pantry over there."

Dawn looked in the direction she nodded to as the small saw was turned on. When Addie put it against the metal on the first shackle, Dawn nearly told her not to do it, but then the heavy weight hit the floor. "That was easy."

Cutting off the other shackle on her ankle was just as quick, but the one at her neck took a bit longer. Not that it was any thicker, but Addie was afraid of cutting her. Dawn told her she'd gladly leave it on herself just to be able to walk around without tripping over the chain, but an hour after starting, Dawn was free.

She wanted to shift and run free. Do something that she'd not been able to do for over two years. Her other self seemed to know that she was free as well, and moved along her skin like it was ready to be out. Dawn calmed her by saying that they would run as much as they wanted soon.

Addie told her she'd be back in the morning, but for Dawn to hide when she saw her car until she saw Addie. Her car was sometimes used by other people, and she didn't want her seen.

"There's a man that works for me—he and his wife really. They are Bill and Carrie Price. He might bring you things when I can't, all right?" Dawn nodded. "Only them. And here's what they look like so you know to trust them."

After showing her the picture of the couple, Addie moved around the house with her, pointing out things that might need a once over and where to find things that were not readily available. Then when they were in the living room again, the furniture now uncovered of the heavy plastic, Dawn turned to her again.

"Why are you doing this? You don't have to, and I'm pretty sure that you have better things to do than to help a runaway, even one as old as I."

Addie nodded and looked around the house before she answered her. "My dad is sick. Dying. He has cancer, and he's been told he only has a few years left at most. I might...would it be all right if I come out here and just unload on you once in a while? Not often, but sometimes?" Dawn nodded. "Then that's why I'm doing it...along with the fact that no one should have to be treated as you've been without someone helping them out."

"I don't know what to say. I mean, thank you seems so little for what you've given me." Addie nodded and turned to the door again. "This thing you can do with my mind...can you do it to everyone?"

Yes. I'll check on you once in a while this way too. You won't know it, but I'll do it. Her voice echoed in her mind, and Dawn thought it wonderful. *You should be able to do it as well. Just think of me and we can talk. You can tell me when you're having troubles this way as well.*

I've never done this before. Addie laughed, and so did Dawn. It was strange to hear the sound coming from her mouth too. *You'll be safe now, right? I mean, I don't want anyone to hurt you now that you've been so kind to me.*

I will, and you will too. Don't come out of the house, or wherever you decide to hide, unless you see that it's me. Dawn asked her how long she could stay there. *For as long as you desire. Forever if you want.*

Dawn nodded, not sure if she could believe her or not. After Addie made her way out to the car, she pulled things from her trunk and handed them to Dawn. What Dawn couldn't carry, Addie sat on the porch. Not even looking into the bags, Dawn had gone into the house to put the first load on the table when she heard the engine roar to life, then gravel crunch in the drive. By the time she came back out to tell her good-bye, Addie was gone.

Unpacking the bags, Dawn was surprised to see all the food. There were things that had to be put in the freezer, and even though she'd not had time to clean it, Dawn put them inside with the plastic bags still around them. Milk and eggs, too, had to be put into the fridge, but she knew that it was going to be the first thing she cleaned.

Pulling out the cleaning supplies that had been in the large pantry, Dawn got to work. While she did this, she thought of all the things she'd have to do before going to bed. It wasn't as daunting as it would have been had she been at her relatives' place, but exciting. Almost fun.

It took her nearly five hours to get the place clean, and that was only the kitchen and the bedroom she was going to use. Crawling into the bed, bathed and with a pretty night gown on, Dawn decided that she'd have to figure out a way to pay Addie back.

For the next few days, she cleaned and aired the house out. There wasn't any television, but she didn't care. Dawn hadn't watched much before and doubted she'd miss it now. Mr. Bill came by twice...once with his wife just to meet Dawn, then the second time to bring her more food. She had so much that she spread it out on the counter and just looked at it. And he'd brought her a loaf of homemade bread, as well as some scones. Dawn cried for an hour after he left, not believing that someone could be so nice to her.

Dawn started making lists of things she needed to pay Addie back for. First was food and clothing. Then there was the cell phone she had for emergencies. Bill told her he'd call her when he was coming out so she'd know to watch for him. He'd brought her a radio, too, and some music to listen to. All in all, Dawn had it better than she'd ever had in her entire life. And all thanks to a perfect stranger.

Dawn was happy...happier than she'd ever thought she'd be. As she sat down to her meal, the first in her wonderfully clean house, she dined on the bread and some soup while classical music played softly in the background. After that she went into the yard, stripped down, and turned into her wolf. As she ran deep into the woods, ever careful of her surroundings, Dawn knew that if she had to go back now after her taste of freedom, she surely would die.

CHAPTER 1

Present day

Ellis decided that if one more thing went wrong today he was surely going to use the nail gun he was holding right now on someone. If he could ever get the fucking thing to work. He stretched his neck again, trying his best to get the stiffness out of it, but there was just no hope for it. He was going to be in a shitty mood for the rest of his life. Ellis glanced up when he heard someone clear their throat, and wasn't surprised—not really—to see his dad there.

"Don't even start." His dad said nothing, which for some reason pissed him off more. "Christ, I'm in charge here. Did everyone forget that when they woke the hell up this morning?"

"No. I'm pretty sure they know who the one who yells at them is. You got a perfect handle on that." His dad came to where Ellis was standing and watched him work on the gun. "What's it doing?"

"Nothing. Not a damned thing. It's loaded, the power is on, but it's simply not fucking working." The hand to the back of his head did nothing to improve his sour mood.

"Dad, perhaps it would be better if you, like the rest of the people I know, just left me alone."

"It's unplugged." Ellis looked at his dad, then down at the gun. It was plugged in. He'd set the extension cord to it himself. "Won't work because there is no power to it. How many times I gotta tell you to check the simplest problems first?"

Mumbling to himself, he slammed the gun down to go and prove to his dad that it fucking had power. As soon as he got to the junction, he simply sat down on the nearest roll of conduit. Not only was it unplugged, but someone had coiled up the extension cord into a neat circle and put it on the floor next to several others. His dad came into the room with him and leaned against the wall, just staring at him for several minutes before Ellis finally spoke.

"I've been having trouble sleeping. And when I do sleep, it's to have the same dream over and over. A woman. I can't save her from someone and she's killed. It's all my fault too, and she tells me that right before she bleeds out." Dad asked him who she was. "I don't know her. Never see her face or anything about her other than that she's tall and slim."

Ellis thought of the woman in the woods, the one he'd been trying to find for nearly a month of going up there on weekends and coming back exhausted and pissed. It was her. He had no idea why he knew it was, but as surely as he was sitting here, it was her.

"It's your mate." He nodded. "You know this? And you don't have a clue who she is? Ellis, you have to find her. It's making you crazy."

"Don't you think I know that?" He looked around when he realized how loud he'd been. "I know that's who it is. But what the hell am I supposed to do if I can't find her? And trust me, I'm trying."

"Where did you see her first? In your dreams, where is she?" Ellis looked at his dad, then back at his feet. He was ashamed to admit even to him that he'd fucked this up. "Ellis, I'm going to help you."

Before he could answer him, Jarrett came in the room with them. He was dressed for work, wearing his new polo shirt with the name Emerson Computer blazed over the left pocket, along with the logo that Jack had made for him just recently. He looked like something was wrong, and Ellis stood up to go and kill whatever was bothering him.

"I need your help. Well, Addie does. I have...it's the strangest thing I've ever asked you to do." Ellis doubted that. When they'd been kids, Jarrett was the one who usually came up with a plan that would get them all in hot water. "I need just you and a couple of men you can trust to go to a house on the property at the big house."

Ellis knew every bit of the property up at the house that Jarrett and Addie kept to get away. There was a pool house, a barn that held nothing more than a few pieces of lawn equipment yet was big enough to hold a plane, and a shed closer to the house that looked like it had been built before the house.

"Which one?"

Jarrett looked around, then stepped more into the room they were in. He looked around again and had him and Dad doing the same.

"It's nearly at the end of the property, like butt up against the end. A woman lives out there that doesn't like people overly much. Addie said she's lived there for nearly eight years, and she's been all alone all this time. But something happened to the roof, and it needs to be fixed." Ellis nodded, thinking of the three people that he'd send up there. He'd had enough of roaming the woods up there to know that the woman he was looking for was long gone. "She asked that you go too."

"I have a business to run." Jarrett nodded but said nothing. "I have to finish up here, Jarrett. I'm only three days ahead of schedule now. I need to be here to make sure that my men get the bonus."

"Yeah, I guess Sloan is wanting you to go up there too, and said that she'd give you an extension of a week. She also said that she didn't think you'd need it, but she's offering." Ellis knew when he'd been had, and this was it big time. "It's important to Addie, and when it's important to her, it's important to me."

"Pussy." Jarrett nodded and smiled. "I really don't want to do this; you know that, right?"

"I do, but Addie said it was important to her, and when you have a mate, you'll understand how it becomes important to you." Ellis didn't look at his dad, but he knew he was staring a hole in the back of his head. "She said to make use of the house as you want. There is staff there to wait on you hand and foot. But make sure that whoever you take is going to be trustworthy. I guess this woman, whoever she is, has someone chasing her."

Ellis said he'd go. And he didn't have any problem picking out the three men that would go with him. The problem he had was that his dad wanted to go. Telling him no was going to be too much effort, so he said he could go as well as part of the crew. Their dad could work as well as, if not better than, most of the men working for him. Ellis went to find Dan to tell him what was going on.

"Good." Ellis cocked a brow at him. "No offense, Emerson, but with the mood you've been in lately, I'll be glad to see the ass end of you for a few days. Might even get this project done if you're not here. Maybe you could, I don't know, get laid or something while you're gone. Might loosen you up a little."

Ellis wanted to be pissed, but he knew his mood and thought perhaps Dan was right. Not about getting laid, but that they might get done sooner. In the last five days, he'd messed up something major twice. Tearing it out to start over was what had put them only three days ahead of schedule and not the desired week.

The plane was ready to go within the hour. They were planning to buy the supplies they needed when they got there, but the men with him had brought their own things they liked to use. His dad had a hammer, a gift from their mom their first Christmas together as man and wife. Billy had a single screwdriver. It was cheap and would more than likely break the first time he set it to a screw, but his kid had given it to him for Father's Day one year, and he'd not had the heart to tell them he had better.

Ellis had a little level, which wasn't much use either. It was barely on point, and when you bumped it, even slightly, it would have five little bubbles in it rather than just the one. But he loved it. It was special to him because, like his dad's hammer, his mom had given it to Ellis. He'd been five, and it had been the best gift he'd gotten that birthday.

As soon as they landed, Bill met them at the airport. He'd come up the week before to see to the house, getting it ready for Easter. They were all coming up in two weeks to stay there and to celebrate the holiday as a family.

Everyone was excited because it really was an amazing house.

"I've made arrangements with Miss Dawn. She's left the area and will await you all leaving before she returns. She is not much of a people person." Ellis nodded and decided that he might enjoy living that way, all alone, with no one to bother him. "You have been made aware that no one is to mention the house or where it is, correct?"

"Yes. I had a long conversation with Addie just before we left. She said that for eight years, this woman has been on her own without much contact with anyone." Bill nodded, and Ellis could see the sadness on his face. "Is she running from an abusive husband?"

"No. But the person chasing her is related to her." Bill turned to the woods before he spoke again. "She's a shifter and has been sorely abused, Ellis. I think…when I first met her all those years ago, I thought her to be much younger than she was. Silly she was, dancing about the house showing us what she'd done to make it right. But I found out from Miss Addie that she'd been chained to the wall, a shackle around her neck and legs so that she couldn't leave or shift. It nearly made her insane with it. Then she was free and it made her…giddy, I suppose would be a good word for it. But she's changed so much now."

Ellis waited for him to continue, but when he didn't, Ellis asked. He didn't want to take his men into a situation that was going to get any of them hurt. But Bill only shook his head and told him it wasn't that.

"She's lonely, I think. But I doubt she understands that is all it is. When I go to see her, bring her things that she might need, she talks a mile a minute, yet seems to want me gone at the same time. I fear, sir, that she's becoming afraid of her own shadow. She talks of a man that comes to the woods searching, and she said he'll find her soon enough."

Ellis had no idea why, but he knew it was him. The woman was talking about him. He never thought...never really cared that he might frighten someone else when he'd been up there all the time. Finding the woman that haunted him was his only goal. And he'd never thought of what it might do to others around the area to see him or to smell his wolf.

Going to the site was a job. Traveling by truck through the dense forest had him so beaten around in the truck that when he finally got to the house, he was ready to shift and take care of the bumps and bangs he'd gotten. But they'd had to come from the backend of the property and not the front so as not to disturb the drive in. This was getting stranger and stranger all the time.

~~~

Dawn watched them from her perch on the tree. Only recently had she been playing with shifting into other animals, and had found that the big falcon was her favorite, next to the wolf. She loved the freedom of them all. And she also liked being able to change what she looked like.

They were walking around the side of the house where the tree had come down on her room during the storm yesterday. The big man looked like he was in charge, and an older man seemed to be ordering the people around. She could see that they were related because they looked like each other a great deal. The two men with them seemed to be hanging onto their every word, so she knew that things would be taken care of soon.

Flying to the big house, she made her way to the room that Bill had said she could use. The window being open made it easier for her to move in and out of the house without anyone seeing her, and she liked that just fine.

Dawn knew that she was being somewhat of a recluse. Well, really, she supposed that she was. People made her nervous, and when she made her way into town, which she did weekly now, she tried to avoid them as much as possible.

Going into town to get her own food had been an experience. The first time she'd done it a few years ago, she'd been terrified out of her mind that someone would tell her aunt and uncle where she was. But no one had noticed her or, for that matter, even looked at her twice. She'd done her shopping, buying things that she couldn't grow, and then left. She'd been making herself do it weekly, even if it was to just get her mail.

Shifting again, she stood in the big bedroom and looked around. It was lovely, the colors bright and friendly. Books were neatly stacked on the shelves, and she saw a few that she'd not read yet. Making a mental note to ask Bill if she could take them back with her, she sat on the chair and opened her computer.

Dawn had been very successful with her vegetable garden for years now. She hadn't been at first, only growing enough to make her frustrated, and even then the vegetables weren't all that good when she'd cooked them. The second year, Carrie had come to help her get started, showing her what to plant, where, and how much fertilizer to put on each plant. She'd been just sticking things in the ground where she had room and had not just crowded things out, but had over-fertilized them as well.

Ordering seeds that she'd like to plant, Dawn closed down her computer and sat watching the woods behind the house. Making a note to tell Bill that the seeds would be coming here cash on delivery, Dawn laid out the money she'd put aside for the order. She thought about the dreams she'd been having about the man in the woods.

He'd been in her thoughts a great deal. Not that she'd ever seen him very much, but she could smell him when she went to the woods. He was a wolf, someone that she was sure had been hired by her uncle to find her. But there was something so calming about him. He was lovely to look at, and he seemed…intense was a good word.

Dawn had gone to see her relatives a few times recently…not to see them, but to see if they were still around. Neither of them seemed to be working, and the house was in such bad repair that Dawn was surprised to see that it was still standing after last night. But it was, and there didn't seem to be any damage done to it that would have made it any worse. The cars were now overgrown with grass that had been there since she'd been brought to them. And the two recliners that had always been on the porch had been replaced with lawn chairs.

As far as she could see neither of them worked, but they were living well. When she'd been there that morning, before coming here, she'd seen them bringing in groceries that filled the back of their truck from front to back. And it was not all food. There were cases of pop, as well as lots of microwaveable foods…something Dawn never ate even being alone all the time. She knew that when she'd lived there that they had gotten a food stamp card, and supposed that nothing much had changed with that.

And she knew that they were still looking for her.

Two weeks ago she'd been in the little grocery store that she used when her aunt walked in. Dawn wanted to run and never stop, but Aunt Neva had walked right by her as if she'd not known who she was. It didn't occur to her until later that she more than likely wouldn't have known her, because Dawn had colored her hair to look older, and had lightened her eyes with contacts.

"Have you seen this girl?" The picture of her from high school was shown to the cashier, who, of course, shook her head. "It's my niece and she's been gone for five years. I really want to find her."

"I'm sorry. I don't know her." Aunt Neva turned to her then, and Dawn was sure she was going to grab her when she showed her the picture. Dawn stared at it for several seconds before she shook her head and handed it back.

"She's not right in the head. It's why we want to find her. Can't have her being that way and out on her own, you know." Dawn didn't say anything, but it didn't seem to bother Aunt Neva. "Them social people want us to have her sign off on some papers or we're going to stop getting her check each month. It was hard enough on us when they stopped sending us her inheritance when she was eighteen."

"She has...maybe she's taken her money and is living in another country." Aunt Neva shook her head and said she was too stupid. "I see. And her inheritance? That'll be yours again when she signs the papers? Wait, there was an inheritance?"

"You're awfully nosey." Dawn backed from her and bumped into the counter behind her. "You know her, don't you? Or you know where she is."

"I don't know her. I swear I don't. I was just curious is all." Aunt Neva glared at her for several minutes, and Dawn felt her body, her wolf, shift under her skin. But before she could leave, make excuses and get out of there, Aunt Neva spoke again.

"I guess I don't need to worry none about you. As old as you are, you'll probably be dead in a bit anyway." Aunt Neva lunged at her and said boo, and, of course, Dawn jumped back again, knocking over a big display of Valentine cards.

After her aunt left, she helped the woman clean up the mess, telling her how sorry she was about it. The clerk told her not to worry about it, that it happened all the time.

"She's been in here every week for years asking about that poor girl. I wouldn't want to be found by her either. And that man? He's a prick." Dawn said nothing, but her mind was working hard. "They're the type of people that will drain her dry while the whole time telling her how much of a burden she's been to them."

Dawn looked at the girl now. She'd been right about it all. Not just the burden part, but she'd gotten her aunt and uncle pegged as well. But instead of asking her how she knew, she stood up and moved to the counter to pay for her things.

Money had never been something that she'd thought about when living with them. She knew that it was necessary and that it was nice to have, but it wasn't until she started making her own that she started to really know its worth. The first year that Bill had bought all the vegetables that she'd grown and couldn't do much with, she'd thought he was being charitable to her. Then the second year he'd asked her if he could take them to the local store to sell. It had been so much money that she'd hoarded it in the event that she never got any again. Now, years later, she was making enough selling to the local stores and a few other places that she could spend a little extra on herself if she wanted. And she'd been able to send a nice gift to Addie when she'd married a few weeks ago.

The noise in the yard had her looking out the window. They were all there, the two men and their crew, plus Bill. He was telling them about something to do with the house. She then watched as he went to his car. When he left her and them, Dawn actually panicked a little. Now what?

The older man came into the house; the rest left again. She was still trying to think what to do, where to go, when she realized that they were going to be living here too. Dawn had no idea why she didn't think of that before. Where else would they rest while her house was being taken care of? When Dawn went to the window, ready to find another place to stay, Addie touched her mind.

I thought you'd like to know the people who are fixing your house. The older gentleman is Cash Emerson. He's my father-in-law. And you couldn't find a nicer, sweeter man. The man in charge is Ellis Emerson, my brother-in-law and one of the middle sons to Cash. He's very nice and owns the construction company that's doing the work. The others are Billy and Andy Coltrane. They're nice young men that are cousins, but I'd swear that they're brothers the way that —

I need to leave here. Addie told her she didn't. *But they're going to tell them where I am, and they'll come here and mess things up for you. You know they will. I told you what that woman said.*

They won't be able to get to you, Dawn. I told you I'd keep you safe so long as you listened to me. Now do that. Those men out there are not going to harm you. It would do you a world of good if you were to go out and introduce yourself to them. Not a single one of them would do a thing against you. I promise. Dawn was shaking her head as Addie continued. *Take a deep breath and listen to me. They're not going to harm you. They won't let your aunt and uncle come there to take you either. You're as safe with them as you are with me.*

Shifting, Dawn took to the skies. Addie kept talking to her, telling her how safe she was, but she wasn't and she'd never be. Going to her house, she went in through the opening that the tree had made and shifted again, this time into her wolf. It wasn't until she was ready to go out again, take to the woods, that she realized she wasn't alone.

CHAPTER 2

Ellis stared at the she-wolf and didn't move. He knew that she was upset. The fur along her back was standing on end and her canines were showing. And if that wasn't indicator enough, she was growling low in the back of her throat.

"Calm down. I'm only here to see how big the other window is so I can match them up." As he made his way along the wall to the doorway, she paced him. "I'm Ellis Emerson. My dad and I are here to work on the house. I know that you live here. I can smell you. I'm not going to hurt you."

He felt Addie touch his mind, and he told her now was not a good time. *Her name is Dawn Whitfield. She's terrified that you're going to tell her aunt and uncle that she's there.*

Nodding, he looked at the beautiful wolf. "I'm talking to Addie. She said that you're hiding from an aunt and uncle. They're not coming anywhere near you so long as I'm alive. She told me your name is Dawn Whitfield."

She wants you to leave her alone. As you might guess, this is the woman you were told about. I'm worried for her, Ellis. Just don't let anything happen to her.

I won't. Addie, did you send me here because you knew what she was to me? Ellis waited for his sister-in-law to answer, and when she didn't, he knew he had his answer. *How long have you known that I was looking for her?*

The moment I touched her all those years ago.

Ellis staggered back just a little, and Dawn moved toward him. He wasn't sure if she was going to attack him or not, but he let his own wolf take him just as she tried to move by him, quicker than him because of his clothing tangled around him. He took off after her just as she leapt out of the broken wall. Ellis was pissed, but this was more important to him right now.

She was easy to follow now. First of all, she was hardly covering her tracks; and secondly, his wolf was bigger and he was a little faster than her. When he caught her, tackled her to the ground, she came up fighting so hard and so fast that it was all he could do not to hurt her. He sank his teeth into her flesh and created a connection so that he could talk to her.

Stop it. Her teeth snapped uncomfortably close to his throat, and he had to bite her harder in the shoulder to keep her down. When he pressed his body over hers, Ellis let her struggle until she simply wore herself out. *I'm not going to let you up because I have a feeling that you're not as tuckered out as you are trying to get me to believe.*

I want you to let me go and to get out of my house. Ellis just held her, knowing that as soon as he did let her go she'd either tear him up or she'd run again. And she knew these woods better than he did. *Are you listening to me?*

I am. But I'm not going to do as you want. Not yet at any rate. When she tried again to get from under him, he sank his teeth harder into her and tasted her warmed blood. *You're not going to be harmed by me or anyone with —*

You're hurting me now. He knew that while he might be hurting her a little, she had cut into him much worse today. *Let me up and we'll talk.*

No. I'll talk and you'll listen for now. I want to tell you what you are to me. She struggled again, and he had to work at holding her. *Damn it all to hell, are you always this trusting?*

I don't trust people at all. He could see that and said as much. *How much did they give you to find me? Huh? A lot? I hope you got it up front, because I doubt they have much more than a few hundred dollars to pay you with. Apparently, my social security that they were getting from me ran out when I was eighteen. And there is some sort of inheritance too. From who, I have no idea, but I'm sure you're aware of it.*

I have no idea who you're talking about. And no one offered me anything but room and board to come up here and fix your house for you. She didn't move for several minutes, but he wasn't fooled. *My brother is married to Addie. She said she wanted us to come up here and repair some damage done by the ice storm yesterday. Did you get hurt?*

No. It scared me when it came crashing in, but I'm just fine. His wolf whimpered just a little in response to her statement. *Let me go, please. I want to go home.*

I can't do that just yet. Do you have any idea what you are to me, Dawn? My mate. She didn't say anything, and he wondered if it worked the same way with shifters as it did with wolves. *You and I are one; our destinies are slated so that we are together for the rest of our lives. I will protect you with my life.*

I don't want your protection. I want to be left alone. I've done well by myself. And I'd very much like to keep it that way.

Ellis let her go, knowing that since he'd tasted her blood she'd not get far from him now. When she stood near him, panting and growling again, he couldn't help but marvel at her beauty.

Will you do me a favor? Will you talk to Addie and ask her what she knows about the two of us? She has known for a long time that you were my mate. She said since the first time she touched you. I only just found out when I saw you. She looked to her left, and he did as well. His dad was coming in the truck. When he looked back at Dawn, he really wasn't surprised to see that she'd left him. Now to tell his dad.

"Son?" Ellis stood up and shook out his fur. He wasn't hurt, at least nothing more than his pride. "What's happened around here? Why do I smell...is that a female?"

My mate. Ellis waited for that to sink in while he moved to the house. He smiled. His dad laughed and followed. *Is there something in the truck I can wear? I'm sort of without clothing.*

"Sure. Sure. I had that man of Addie's throw some of our things in there when he was loading them at the house." A small bag was tossed at him. "Your mate, huh? Where is she? When you gonna bring her home so I can welcome her to the family?"

Ellis waited to answer until he was dressed. The laces in his boots were shot, but there was always a few extra pair of them in his tool box. The clothing was hot now that he'd shifted, and he left the jacket off while he sat at the table in the kitchen. When his dad sat beside him, Ellis looked at him.

"She's the recluse that Addie told us about. Something about an aunt and uncle trying to find her is why we were never allowed to say anything to anyone about her." His dad nodded and looked around the room too. "Her name is Dawn, Dawn Whitfield, and she's about as trusting as Sloan was when we first got to town. She thinks I've been paid by her aunt and uncle to bring her home."

"I see. And you and her tangled, did you?" Ellis showed his dad his arm where she'd caught him with her paw. "I wouldn't have known a she-wolf, a mate of yours, could do that. Let me clean you up."

He knew that so long as they weren't fully mated that the wounds wouldn't heal. He'd read it somewhere a long time ago when he'd been about seventeen. As his dad cleaned him up, Ellis looked harder around the little house.

The kitchen was spotless. Herbs hung from the long beams, and there were pretty empty bottles that he'd bet were old sitting in the window catching the light. There was a dish in the drainer, as well as a cup, glass, and a single fork. For some reason he couldn't fathom, it made him sad to think how lonely it looked. His own kitchen looked much the same in his apartment.

"There you go." Ellis looked up at his dad as he finished cleaning his wound, knowing that whatever he was going to say was going to be profoundly unhelpful. "You have to find her."

"I know that." His dad sat down. "She's not really interested in my finding her, so it might not be all that easy."

"What's this about her aunt and uncle you mentioned? You think she'd go there to get away from you?" Ellis shook his head. "Well, she'll have to come back here sometime. You can just wait her out. There is more than the one bedroom here that you can use. Not the big house, but it might not be so bad with a mate here."

"Dad, she's not going to come back here so long as I'm here. She doesn't trust me. And Addie knew that she was my mate too." His dad looked at him strangely, then laughed. "This is not funny, damn it."

"She sent you up here on this...this mission of mercy, because she knew that this here girl was your mate and she figured it was about time you got yourself hitched? If that ain't funny, then nothing is." He laughed harder, and Ellis might have hit him had he not been his father. "Yep, that's about as funny a thing as I've heard in a long while. Got yourself a mate that is terrified to no end of you, and you being you."

"What the hell does that mean, me being me?" His dad got up to clean up his mess and was still laughing when he looked in the refrigerator. When he came back with a glass of tea, Ellis wanted to hit him in the head with the little tin he'd unearthed too.

"You learn anything from your brother when he was trying to get Sloan to do what he wanted?" He moaned. "These are some fine cookies, son. You should have yourself one. You won't go hungry with this one, I'm betting."

"Dad." Dad chuckled, and Ellis got up and took the tin and the glass from him. "You're going through her things. Don't you think that's going to piss her off more?"

"More than likely, but you can handle her for me, can't you?" Ellis just stared at him and then left the house. Fuck, nothing was going right, and he was pissed.

Ellis didn't have any idea where she was or what she was doing. For all he knew, she could be staring at him from a tree or watching him from some point on the ground. Either way, she was going to take a lot of convincing to come and talk to him. He reached for Addie.

I need your help. What do I do to convince her that I'm not going to turn her over to them? Addie didn't answer right away, and Ellis felt the pain of losing Dawn harder than he'd ever thought possible. *I'll do whatever you tell me to do. I…she's hurting, and there is nothing I can do to convince her that I'm here for her.*

I will think on it, Ellis. I didn't know until recently how badly they had hurt her. Things were done to her that no child should have had to live with. Daily beatings, verbal and mental abuse. It's a small wonder that since she found me that she has been able to do what she's done. Her mind is tightly guarded; she believes that everyone will turn her over to them, and until the other day, I thought her just afraid. But they really are still looking, and when they find her, I think they'll kill her.

Who are they? And where are they? I won't go and see them, because to do that would sever any trust she might ever have for me, but I'd like to know my enemies. And as of the moment I found her, they became that. He looked at the woods. There were so many places she could be. *Addie, did you really know all this time what she was to me?*

Somewhat. I knew that it was a man that I would trust as I would my own husband someday. But when I saw you in her future, it wasn't a man that I saw but a dog…a wolf, I know now. And I never knew for sure it was you until she contacted me about the wall coming down. She laughed a little. *She was so afraid when she called me. Swearing that the walls were coming down on her head and that a cannon had gone off. Is it bad? The house, is it bad?*

No. Some structural damage to the wall. The window will need to be replaced and the roof rebuilt. There is some water damage done to the flooring, but nothing that a good carpet cleaning won't fix. He turned and looked at the house. *It's in great shape. She's kept it beautifully maintained. And if you only ever entered from the rear, you'd think she had a crew working for her to keep up this yard.*

She has a massive garden, too. A few years ago, Bill made contact with one of the local stores to buy her excess from her, and she has been selling to them ever since. I managed to convince her that I had no further use for the tractor in the barn or she'd still be cultivating the sucker with a hoe. She paused. *Her mom died some time ago in prison. I didn't know her, but of her. She murdered a cop in a bank robbery. I guess after Dawn's father died, there was no income and she was desperate, and that's why she turned to robbery. The uncle is her mom's brother, and his wife, Neva, is a piece of work. You'll hate her on sight. His name is Basil Combs. If her mom was married to Dawn's dad, I have no idea who he is. Just the last name Whitfield. The aunt and uncle live about a mile from the end of our property line. The house sits a little back from the road, and has three cars in the front yard that have weeds taller than them around them. Don't go there alone, Ellis. If you do, there is no telling what might happen to you. I had someone go there a few years ago to buy them out, and he told me he'd never go back.*

I need to fix this for her. Whatever it takes. She told him that she'd help too. *I'm going to try some things here. I don't know that they'll work, but I'm going to shamelessly use my father.*

Her laughter made him smile. *He's a perfect person to break the ice. I just love that man. And he did a great job raising you guys, too.*

I think so too, but don't tell him that. His head is big enough already. Ellis looked around the yard and then thought of something that would have brought Hunter's wife Sloan out of the house quicker than anything. *I'm going to help her in her gardening.*

I don't know, Ellis. She's pretty…ah, I see. Well, good luck with that. I'm going to make some inquiries to see what I can find out about her family. There is going to be hell to pay now that you've found her.

Ellis looked around again. He had no idea whether or not she was close by, but he knew that he could reach out to her. Thinking of how to word it so as not to piss her off too much, he grinned.

My dad is here. He works with my other sister-in-law in her garden. Since you have to be away from your home and garden, I'm going to have him work the ground for you. I know that pea planting season is about here. Ellis started to go to his dad when Dawn answered him.

You most certainly will not have anyone working in my garden. I have a system, and he will mess it up. Ellis moved to his dad and started telling him what he wanted him to do and why. Of course, he was all for it. *Did you hear me? I said not to have him do anything to my garden.*

I heard you, but you have to let me do something for you. Ellis watched as his dad went to the big barn. *You should know that he's gotten really good at driving a tractor. He's not hit anything in a long while.*

Ellis made his way to the house again. If she came to help his dad or not, he thought it best to let his dad handle it. One thing Ellis knew about his dad, he was the biggest-hearted man he knew, and he'd do anything to help him help Dawn.

~~~

Dawn came out of the woods just as her tractor was making its way out of the barn. The elderly man sitting atop it looked like he'd been born to be there, but that didn't mean she was going to let him in her garden. As she stood in front of him, he stopped the tractor but didn't turn it off.

"I can do this." He cupped his hand over his ear as if he couldn't hear her, and she shouted again. "I can do this. Please just get down and let me do it."

As the tractor engine turned off, she waited for him to get down. The nerve of these people thinking she needed their help with gardening. But the man smiled at her, and she found herself smiling back.

"He thinks I can charm you into about anything." Dawn looked up at the house, then back at the man. "My name is Cash. My son is Ellis. He told me to see if you'd come out of the woods and let me help you. Thinks you and I can hit it off, and then you might not hate him so much."

"I don't hate him. I don't even know him." Cash nodded but didn't say anything more. "I can do my own gardening, thank you very much."

"No doubt you can, but I'd really like to help. Lifting and toting are hard on an old man, and this way I can earn my keep." Dawn looked at him. The man had on a pair of boots that cost more than all the clothing in her house. Earning his keep was going to be expensive, she thought. "You gotta let me do this, child. It's the most fun a man can have working with a pretty girl like you."

"I'm far from pretty, so keep your blarney to yourself." His roar of laughter made her blush. And when two of the other men stopped working to look at them, she waved them back to work. "Mr. Cash...you are going to be difficult about this, aren't you?"

"I am." At least he was honest. "I want to help you. I need to help. Ellis there is your mate. And that means that we're family."

"I don't have what it takes to be a mate. I have to…Addie gave me some information on being a mate to someone. She gave me all kinds of books about everything, but that one stuck in my head because it said that things would be wonderful once you found the other half of your soul." He nodded and smiled at her. "I'm a shifter, Mr. Cash. I know that shifters are considered to be the scourge of the world in the paranormal community, and me—"

"Where on earth did you read that?" His voice was hard and she took a step back from him. Fear of being hit had her suddenly afraid of him. "I'm not gonna ever hurt you, child. Not ever. But that's just bull malarkey. Whoever…that's just the dumbest thing that I've ever heard. You want to know who is scourge? I'll tell you. It's the person that wrote that down for you to read. Give me his name. I'm gonna go and find him right now and set him to rights. Scourge of the…well, I'm going to show him scourge."

Dawn laughed. It had been so long since she'd laughed like this that she was surprised at how good it felt. And when she looked at Cash, he had the strangest look on his face.

"You do get worked up, don't you?" He nodded and told her she was beautiful. "No. But I thank you for that. And the laugh."

"Where do we start on this garden of yours?"

She didn't have it in her to turn him down again. There was something so incredibly charming about him that she found herself wanting to spend more time with him, and if he wanted to work with her in the garden, she'd let him.

"I have to get the ground ready for the peas. It's nearly time to get them in the ground." He told her that Sloan had everything ready to go in late fall, furrows ready and all. "I might do that, but I grow pumpkins and gourds then to sell in town."

"Sell it, do you? Sloan just gives it all to the pack house. Helps out, too, when you have a pack the size that Hunter has. He's my oldest boy. He and Sloan are married and expecting my first granddaughter in a few months. End of May." Cash got back up on the tractor when she showed him where to plow. Then before starting it back up, he asked her to move back. "I'm not bad at driving this thing, but I don't want to take any chances that I might hurt you. Stand on back there by that tree and I'll work this here magic for us."

She watched him plow and was impressed at how precise he was about it. The rows were neater than hers had ever been, and he did the entire garden in about half the time she would have. When he turned the engine off again and hopped down, she followed him into the barn to get what they'd need to get started.

Before she knew it, they were working the ground like they'd been doing it together their entire lives. And he wasn't a gabber box either, only asking her an occasional question about something or telling her what he and Sloan did about whatever it was, and asking her advice on things she actually had an opinion on.

Her belly growling made her realize that they'd been at this for hours. When she went into her house to fix lunch, she found Ellis standing on a ladder without a shirt on, tearing down the broken ceiling. Swallowing twice, she turned her back on him and could have sworn she heard him chuckle, but he never spoke to her as she tried to think what she came in there for. It wasn't until Cash entered and reminded her that she set to work.

CHAPTER 3

Ellis watched her out of the corner of his eye as he set the boards. Billy was using the nail gun, and he was nervous about Ellis not using it instead of him. When he put the gun to the board to pull the trigger, Billy shifted on his seat and the gun moved just enough to have the nail no longer pointed to the wood. The pain knocked Ellis to the floor.

"I'm sorry, boss. I'm sorry. Christ, I done killed you." Ellis growled low and tried to stand, but there was a person sitting on his chest. Looking up at Dawn, he decided to be still for now.

"Let me look." He moved his hand off the injury. The nail was about three quarters of the way into his flesh, and he had to look away. "Christ. Does it hurt?"

He looked at her and could see that she was afraid for him. "Not too much. It's more my pride than anything. But if you could shut Billy up from apologizing, I'd really appreciate it."

She snapped at Billy to shut up and go outside, and the blessed silence had him thanking her. "No problem. He was bothering me as well. We have to take this out. I'm not sure I can do it without hurting you more."

"Will you kiss me and make it all better?" He was kidding, but the look on her face made him wish that he'd chosen his words better. "I'm kidding, Dawn. I hurt badly now, so if you want someone else to do it, that's fine. But I trust you."

"I'll need pliers." He nodded and yelled for his dad. "Mr. Cash, do you think you can help me with this?"

"I don't...darling, I couldn't even help them boys out when they bloodied their lips scuffing with each other." Ellis looked at his dad. He wasn't telling the truth, and when he winked at him, Ellis could have gotten up and kissed his dad. "I can assist you all you need, but just don't ask me to do anything like you're going to be doing."

"I'll need those pliers and some towels." Dawn looked at Ellis. "Are you going to knock me off if I hurt you?"

"Never." He put his good hand over hers as she held a towel to his bleeding hand. "I might cuss up a storm, but I won't hurt you on purpose."

She nodded and took the things she'd asked for from his dad. Taking a deep breath, she uncovered the wound. Ellis felt his belly jump when he got a really good look at it.

The nail had entered his palm and was sticking out the other side. He knew that it must have missed the bones there because he could still move his fingers. But it was painful. When she told him that she was going to count to three and then pull, Ellis braced himself. When she counted first one, then two, she jerked the nail from his hand.

Sitting up, he unseated her off his chest and she landed with a hard punch to his groin. When the pain there took over the pain in his hand, he put it around her waist and brought her to his body. The urge to bite her was huge, but Ellis only bit his lip as she held him. When she lifted her head, he looked down at her face and felt his heart break for her.

"Honey, it's all right. I swear. My nuts are sore, but my hand is okay." When she started to shift off him, he held her there. "Moving now will only make it worse."

She sat very still, and he watched her face. His cock was filling, and when she shifted over him again, he groaned. Then she looked at him with a cocked brow.

"You're not hurting at all." He nodded and smiled. "What do you think you're doing? I'm not stupid, you know."

"Yes, I know that. But you really did hurt my manly parts. And if having you sit on top of me makes them less painful, then you can't begrudge a man that." She started to shift off him again and then stilled. He felt his wolf move over his skin when she stiffened. "What is it?"

"Someone is coming."

He heard it then. Someone was driving down the drive, and he pushed her off him and stood up. Helping her up, he moved her toward the wall and told her to stay there. She nodded, but he could see the terror on her face.

"No one is going to hurt you. I promise. Just stay here until I come for you." He started to leave her, but she pulled him back. Wrapping the towel around his hand, she let him go, and he moved to the front of the house where the car was just pulling to a stop.

His dad and Billy were standing on the porch when he came out of the house. A man, huge and sloppy, came out of the driver's side of the car, and the woman in the passenger side only stood by the opened door. Andy came out right after he did, and he noticed that not one of his crew looked like they were ready to welcome their guests with open arms.

"Hi there." Ellis nodded at the man. "We didn't even know this place was back here. How long you been working on this place?"

"What made you come here today?" The man looked over at the woman but said nothing. "There are all kinds of no trespassing signs you had to pass to get here. So, again, why did you come here today?"

"We've been looking for our niece." Ellis didn't move to take the paper that the man was holding out. "Thought maybe she was here so we came back. You haven't seen her, have you?"

"This is private property. Can she read? This niece of yours, can she read?" The man told his dad that she could. "Then perhaps she's got herself a bit more sense than you do to come onto property that doesn't belong to her."

"You're not very friendly, are you?" His dad told him he wasn't to people he didn't invite on his property. "You own this then? Good to know. But in case she does come around, we'll be coming to fetch her. She's not right in the head and we have to have her under close watch all the time. So, if you see her, just give us a call and we'll—"

"You never did answer my son. What the hell are you doing here?" The man looked like he was ready to come up on the porch and hit his dad. He even slammed his door shut and made his way to the front of his car. Andy stepped off the porch, as did Billy, and the man would have been stupid not to realize that they were going to kill him if he took another step. "I want you to get on back in your car, turn your asses around, and get out of here. You ever come back here again, I will make it so you never trespass again. You hear me?"

"You threatening me, old man?" Ellis stepped down and walked to the man. He was glad when he took several steps back, as Ellis was able to lean over him when he fell back against his car. "I was just kidding him. Can't a man have a joke among friends?"

"You're not our friend, and as you've been told several times already, this is private property and you are not welcome." The man nodded, and then when Ellis backed up enough for him to slide from in front of him, he walked the man to his door. "No one is here but us. And in the event you didn't get it, we like our privacy. Come here again and I will shoot you."

The man got into his car and turned it around. He was pulling away when the woman flipped Ellis off. Ellis laughed as they peeled out of the drive and left. He looked at Billy and Andy.

"Go and put up a barrier at the end of this drive. Make it deep and impossible to be moved." Andy nodded. "When you have that done, I want you to speak to the pack nearby and let them know what we've done and what we've run into. They knew we were going to be here, and Addie let them know a long time ago about someone staying here."

As they took off to do what he'd told them, he made his way to the porch. His dad was leaning against the post and looked a little nervous. Ellis was nervous too. Those two would be back, and the next time they'd be ready to fight.

Telling his dad to contact Hunter and let him know what was going on, Ellis went into the house. Dawn was standing where he'd left her, but she was crying, and her body was as tight as a drum. Touching his hand to her arm, she whimpered a little, and he wanted to pull her into his arms and hold her. But he was afraid that she'd break.

"That was my uncle and aunt." He nodded and took a step closer to her. "They are still looking for me. After all this time. And I'm not crazy."

"No, you're not. But they are if they think they can come back here and make you upset." She looked up at him, and Ellis ran his fingers gently down her cheek. "I won't let them get to you, honey. And neither will the rest of us."

"He's a mean man. He beat me and chained me to the wall. I had a shackle around my neck so that I couldn't shift." Her tears began to fall, and Ellis stepped closer to her. "Uncle Basil put them around my ankles, too. Then he took great pleasure in telling me that if I shifted with them on, they would sever my feet."

Ellis finally pulled her to him. He held her to his chest while she cried, great sobs that made him want to hunt down her relatives and tear out their throats. When his dad came into the kitchen where they were, he turned his back to them but didn't leave.

"Hunter said that if you need him to call, and Addie is on her way up. She said that she has some information that you can use against this guy. And Shawn is going to come as well. It seems that your aunt and uncle have been receiving monthly checks that belong to you, Dawn." His dad laughed a little. "That girl can sure get her panties all done up when someone tries to take advantage of her family."

"I should just try to find somewhere else to live." It sounded very good to Ellis, but he didn't think she'd appreciate him asking her to come stay with him. "I knew that this was too close to them and they'd find me someday."

"We're not going to let them run you off. Hell's bells, I just helped you put peas in the ground. A man don't just walk away from peas." Ellis nearly pointed out that he hated peas, but he turned then and looked at her. "That uncle of yours.... Did he...? What did he do to you that you're so fired-up scared of him?"

She looked up at Ellis, and he could see what it was costing her to speak. So when she pulled away from him, Ellis pulled her back. When she didn't struggle with him, he watched her face while she spoke to Dad.

"At first it was all right. I was there for about a year before he hit me the first time. He'd lost his job, you see, and there had to be cutbacks, he said. When I pointed out that I already did a lot of the jobs, he said I was going to have to take over and he knocked me off the chair. I shouldn't have said anything. He was under stress, I thought. But as the months, then years, went by, things got worse. The beatings were...just that. Beatings." She leaned into Ellis now, her head resting on his chest, and Ellis looked at his dad while she continued. "I had such plans when I turned eighteen. I was going to leave. I was an adult and it was my right, as such, to leave. But the morning that I turned eighteen, I shifted for the first time. It was...it was the most wonderful feeling in the world. I felt free."

"You didn't know you was a shifter?" She turned and shook her head at Dad, then went to the cabinets and began pulling things down from them. "Your parents, where are they during this time?"

"My mom was in prison. She killed a police officer. I'm not sure what happened, but she didn't have a gun so far as I knew. I never was able to read about her when I was a child. And now...well, I never really cared to go and look. My dad? I have no idea. He was never around, and Mom never talked about him. Not ever." Dawn began mixing up some of the ingredients on the counter, and it was already making his mouth water. "She was gone for several months before anyone came looking for me. Then I was taken to my aunt and uncle almost immediately."

Ellis sat at the table and watched her. He knew some of what had happened, but not a great deal. "What happened when your relatives saw that you could shift? I bet they didn't take kindly to that."

"No. He...my uncle hit me with the broom first. I snarled back at him." She laughed. "Again, such a wonderful feeling. But he hit me again and again until I passed out. I didn't want to hurt him, so I guess that was to his advantage. When I woke up, there was a shackle around my neck, and it was attached to the floor in the kitchen. Just long enough that I could reach all the appliances and nothing more."

"You were their slave." She nodded at him, and Ellis stood up to get glasses and plates as she started putting sandwiches together. "How long did you have to live like that, Dawn? And how did you escape?"

"It was two years before I managed to get away. But by then he'd put them around my ankles as well. Drugged me or something is all I can figure. I felt sick the night before, and when I woke up, they were on me." She handed him a platter of sandwiches and a bowl of what looked like potato salad. "I don't know why I'm telling you this. But anyway, one night I was cleaning the kitchen and I found a long piece of wire. I had no idea how to pick a lock, but I worked in the dark on the one chaining me to the kitchen for days and days. Then one night it just popped. I had a little stash of money and stuff. Not a lot. I'd been running away weekly up until the chains, so I'd learned what I could carry and what I had to have. This time he didn't find me."

"He'd beat you when you came back?" Dawn nodded at his dad when he spoke. "How badly, baby? How badly am I gonna have to make this man pay for hurting you?"

She toyed with her napkin, and Ellis wasn't sure she was going to tell them. But when she looked at him, her face full of the pain of it, he knew that this man was going to die a horribly slow and painful death.

"They had this set up in the basement. It was to keep me in line, they said. I was tied to the wall, and then my back was exposed. The whip that they used, it was leather and it would bite into my skin like it was trying to come out the other side. And the more I screamed or begged them to stop, the more he'd hit me. Then my aunt would take over when his arm was too tired to go on. After that I'd be cut down and have to clean up the blood that dripped from me before I could go lay down. And even then it wasn't in a bed; it was a blanket on the floor, or sometimes the towel I'd used to clean with in a cage." When Dawn lowered her head, Ellis reached over and lifted it up while she finished telling them. "I wouldn't be able to shift to heal. Didn't even know that I could until I came here. But they knew. There was all kinds of things they knew that kept me from feeling better or even feeling whole."

"They're going to die." She shivered, and he cupped her chin again and pulled her to him. Ellis kissed her then, tasting her for the first time, and then pulled back. He wanted her trust now more than ever.

~~~

As she washed up the dishes after lunch, she thought of the kiss. It had been her very first one, and she was glad that it had been him. She liked Ellis and his dad. Even the other two men that were with them, but she wasn't going to be able to leave here when they did. There was too much at stake, and she wasn't going to drag them into it. Her uncle and aunt were going to find her now; she just knew it.

"Miss Dawn? Ellis wants to know if you need anything from town. We're going in to get some concrete and stuff, and he said you might need some extra stuff with us here." She turned to look at Andy, and he blushed brightly. "He said to tell you that he's going to buy some extra meat and stuff too. We're kinda big eaters."

"You are." She had a list of things she was going to get the next time she was in town and pulled it off the refrigerator now. "I have to add to it. How long before you leave?"

"When you're ready. Mr. Cash is going too. He said he needs to stretch his legs." Andy blushed again. "I think he just needs to flirt a bit. He's a man that does that like he breathes."

Dawn laughed. She had figured that out about Cash. He was incorrigible but sweet. She thought him to be the nicest man she'd ever met. As she added things to her list, she had to think how much money she had. There was some in her stash out in the yard, but she would only use that to run if she had to. But feeding these men was going to be expensive.

Ellis came in just as she was counting out her money. "I'll pay for this." She started to tell him no, he would not, but he continued. "Addie gave me money to feed these guys with, and I'm going to use it. She told me she'd have my ass if I didn't do right by you."

"I can do this." He told her he'd pay if she cooked. "You do know that it was only ham sandwiches and some leftover salad. Not that much."

"I rarely get a good hot cooked meal anymore. I don't have time to do it, and when I do, I'm too tired to even bother. Mostly I eat at the diner, and while that's good, it's not personal." She nodded when he asked her if she knew what he meant. "I love the way you made our sandwiches. And so you know, I think that your honey mustard is the best I've ever eaten. But it was the dessert that I enjoyed the best."

"Dessert? I didn't have any made. I can make some for dinner if you want. I have cherries left over from last year and—"

He pulled her into his arms again, a place where she was beginning to enjoy being. "This dessert." His mouth brushed gently over hers. Then again and again. When he pulled her lower lip into his mouth and nibbled on it, Dawn put her hands on his massive arms to hang on. The next time he pressed his mouth to hers, she moaned with his taste.

His tongue ran along her lips, and when she moved her own to taste him again, he entered her mouth with his tongue and wrapped it around her own. He moved it along her mouth, bringing her tongue into his mouth. And then he sucked hard at it, pulling her deeper still when she wrapped her arms around him. Her body was being lifted, pressed against something hard, and when he rocked into her softness, she tore her mouth from his and cried out with it.

"Come for me, Dawn. Let me taste you when you come for me." Her body seemed to be on the very edge of something profound. And when he rocked into her again, commanding her to let go, she screamed out her release as he bit her in the throat. Then everything went black.

She was only out for a few seconds, but when she woke, he was stroking her back and telling her how sorry he was that he'd hurt her. Dawn wasn't sure that he'd hurt her so much as he'd woken up every part of her body. When she moved back to look at him, he stared at her like he was terrified that he was going to hurt her again.

"I never meant to hurt you." She nodded. "I did, didn't I? I hurt you. Christ, all I wanted to do was kiss you, but you tasted so good…amazing, as a matter of fact…that I wanted more."

"I'm not hurt." He didn't look like he believed her. "I'm not. Really. I'm slightly…that was pretty amazing. Is it always like that with kissing you?"

"No. It's much better." He kissed her again, and she moaned when he rocked into her again. "I want you. I know that you're not sure about me yet, so I want to take it slow, but Christ, Dawn, I want to sink my cock into you and never leave."

Her body reacted to his words as if he'd done just that. She moaned when he buried his nose into her throat again, and she curled her fingers into his hair when he nipped at her tender flesh. She wanted him, too, but wasn't sure it was a good idea to act on it.

"I should let you get back to work." He groaned, and she laughed. When he lifted his head and looked down at her, she felt like she could fall right into his eyes. And she thought that she could love him, and knew that was impossible. Men like this one didn't fall in love with girls like her.

Why not? She felt Addie touch her mind just as Ellis set her on the floor again with a quick, yet satisfying, kiss. He was whistling when he entered the bedroom again. *Why couldn't a man like him love you? You're wonderful and amazing.*

You know why. Addie told her that she didn't. *He's a very wealthy man. And being saddled with a woman like me is not in the cards for him. He needs a woman who can hang on his arm and walk into fancy restaurants and know how to act. I've never even been to a restaurant, much less one that would require me to hang on any part of a man.*

I'm sure you can figure out what to hang on to. Dawn felt her face heat up. *He's nearly in love with you now, Dawn. And you him, I think. And Ellis isn't the type of man that would care what you wore, where you sat, or even what you did for a living as long as you were happy doing them all.*

No man is that nice. I might have lived a very sheltered life for a long time now, but I do know a little about men. Addie snorted. *Well, I think I do anyway. And he's just too nice to want to have to tangle with me and my issues. And my aunt and uncle...they were here today.*

Did he give you to them? Did he mention that he knew where you were? Where you'd been all this time? No, he did not. He protected what was his. And, for that matter, they all did. You are family to us all now, Dawn, and we all will protect you if you need it. There were tears in her eyes as she finished up her dishes. *Dawn, I want you to come back with him for a few days. I'd like for you to meet my family. Our new family.*

They'll find me. She told her that they'd not find her there. *I can't, Addie. I'm afraid that…I'm just afraid.*

I know, love, but you have a wonderful man there now, and I bet you that he's going to keep you safer than anyone you know will.

Dawn had no idea. She was afraid to even go into town when she had to. Going to another state might really be too much. As she put the towel over the drainer to dry out, she went into the yard to finish up her peas. Things were going too fast right now, she thought, and it just needed to slow a little bit so she could think.

Thinking is highly overrated. Dawn thought that Addie was right about that too.

CHAPTER 4

Mike Lateen listened to the man in front of him bitch. He wasn't complaining, because in order to do that, he'd have to have an actual complaint. This man was bitching, pure and simple. When he started going on about how he'd been threatened, Mike sat up higher in his chair. Being the sheriff around here did have some perks. And one of them was to show someone like this prick the error of his ways.

About three weeks ago, the little berg that he lived in had a special election. It was quick and easy, and his name had been a write-in. No one, it seemed, was happy with the previous sheriff or the men who had worked for him. Now he was not just the sheriff, but also the alpha to the pack that he pretty much did everything for, including adding all the money to the coffers. And now this idiot was testing even his limits of patience.

"So you entered property that wasn't yours, knowing that there were signs posted that said it was private property, and are now lodging a complaint because...why again?" The man actually looked like he was going to come across the desk at him. "You want my help, Mr. Combs, then you'll calm your temper."

"I think they have my niece. The one I told you about when you first come into this office. The one that has been missing for all these darned years." Basil looked at his wife, who sort of reminded Mike of a snake in the grass, and smiled at her. "We surely do miss her, our niece, and we want some stuff closed-up. There are policies that she has on her that we can't do nothing with until we have her again. And if she's there and her being not right in the head, we'll get our money coming back to us with the social offices."

"Closure?" The man nodded. "I see. And this niece of yours, is she a kid? I mean, you said to me that she was an adult, didn't you?"

"She'd be about twenty-six, I think." Combs flushed when he must have realized how that sounded. "She's been gone so long that I forget."

Mike knew who she was...knew all there was to know about the woman in question. She wasn't twenty-six, but nearly twenty-eight. And she was just where they thought she was; living in the house on the property of Addison Parker, and had been for a while now. The fact that he'd gotten a call from Addie just today had prepared him for this asshole, and some of the things that he'd been doing that were going to land his ass in prison.

"Did you know that after seven years, you can have her declared dead? If there are policies with her name on them, you can go that route and be done with it." The man looked pissed for several seconds before he finally nodded. "You've done that, haven't you?"

"We done did that. But someone is blocking it. They say that they know she's still alive. Nobody will tell us where she's alive at, but they know she's still breathing."

Mike had a feeling if they found Dawn, she'd not be breathing for very long. "We need to get this stuff settled, and those men are keeping us from finding her. We want you to go out there now and tell them to get moved out so we can have a look-see around."

Mike stood up and put on his hat. He was moving toward the door when he turned back to the Combs. "Well, are you coming or not? I don't have time for this crap, and we might as well get it over with."

They giggled. It was the strangest sound he'd ever heard from a human when these two did it. It was giddy and insane sounding at the same time. And yet they seemed to be...well, he thought them to be the dumbest people he'd ever encountered, and that was saying a great deal. But they were smart enough to know that they needed a body or her to claim her money, and stupid in the fact that they really thought he was going to help them. As he got into his car and them into theirs, he called Addie to let her know what was going on.

"So if you could get in touch with Ellis and the rest of them, I'd appreciate it. I don't want to be handed my ass when I pull up with these fools." She laughed and told him that she was landing now and would be at the house in about ten minutes. "Good to know. Anybody else there with you? That alpha of yours, too?"

"No, Hunter stayed home this time, but I have my attorney as well as a few of his crew. They're none too happy about the turn of events. Oh, and Jarrett of course. He said he'd like to have dinner one night while we're here." Mike told her he'd like that. And a few minutes later, after making some arrangements, he hung up. The shit was about to be sprayed all over somebody, and he was glad it wasn't him.

Mike was pulling into the overgrown drive just as a huge limo pulled in, too. He was smiling when he got out of the car, and when he saw Ellis and his dad sitting on the front porch, Mike tipped his hat at them. This was going to be a lot of fun. He wondered where Dawn was and saw the curtain move in one of the windows, and smiled in her direction. The girl sure was a beauty.

"What's going on here? What did you do?" Mike just looked at Basil when he got out of his car shouting at him. "I...what the heck is going on here? These here people weren't here the other time. That fancy car is somebody from the social office, ain't it? You know that they're hiding her. And that ain't fair. Not fair at all."

"This here woman is Addison Emerson. She owns the property." The man said nothing, but he could tell he knew who she was. "Mr. Emerson is her brother-in-law, and that older man is her father-in-law."

"He never done did tell me who he was when I was here before. What does that matter if they're hiding my niece from us? We want her home so we can get this here part over with. I want this fixed now." Mike turned to Ellis and Cash and shook both their hands when Basil stepped up beside him, nearly bursting with anger. "This here is not a social call. I want justice."

"All right. Ellis, this man is mad that you put up no trespassing signs making it so he can't enter this property without you being legally able to shoot him." Basil blustered, but Mike continued. "He also claims that you're hiding his niece here, and he wants me to run you off this property so he can have a...what did you call it? Oh yeah, he wants to have a look-see. I don't think he's all that trusting of you telling him the truth."

"She's here. I know it. And we want her back." Ellis stood up, and Mike felt his own wolf stir. The man was an alpha, a great one, too. And Mike decided that if it ever came to the point where Ellis wanted his pack, he'd hand it over without a fight. This man, he'd just realized, was stronger than him by a great deal. It was hard for him to fight the urge to bend and pledge to him. "You need to leave here now. We just want to find her and take her back where she belongs. Them social people a long time ago said she was ours to raise as we seen fit."

Addie laughed, and they all turned to her when she continued laughing for several seconds. She sure was a pretty thing, too, and seemed to have that man of hers wrapped around her pretty little finger.

"You must be Basil Combs, and this has to be your wife, Neva. My goodness, the hype about you two is certainly bigger than you really are. Well, not bigger in the sense that you're fat and sloppy, but your bark. You do a lot of that, but you're really no threat, are you?" Basil asked her what the heck that meant. "It means that you talk a lot, but it's just talk, just bark. But I have a bite that you'll feel for a good long time if you do not get off my land right now and go back to your hovel and leave my family alone."

"You can't tell me what to do. You might have all the money in the world, but I don't have to listen to you. I done told you, them social people said—"

Shawn stepped forward and pressed a thick envelope into Basil's chest. Mike thought for sure he was paying him off, but when Basil opened the envelope and a sheaf of legal looking documents fell out, Mike laughed too.

"What the heck is this supposed to be?"

"You're being sued, Mr. Combs. Trespassing, just to start with. Threatening an officer for another reason. Then there is—"

"I did no such a thing. This here is just me coming here to find my niece." Mike crossed his arms over his chest while Basil continued to spout off anything in his empty head. "I want her back. Do you hear me? I demand that you make these people do as I want right now, 'cause I got me a temper and I don't want it to go off on you."

"You just threatened him by telling him that you've a temper and it might go off if you don't get your way. What would you call that if not a threat?" Basil looked confused, but Shawn continued before the man burst something in his head. "Even if your niece was here, she's well within her rights as an adult to live where she wants with whoever she wants. You are no longer responsible for her or anything about her."

"She's nuts." Everyone looked at Neva when she spoke for the first time. "Right before she left us, she told us that she could be an animal if she wanted. And when she was this thing, she was going to come back and tear our throats out. We have to have her back to keep us safe."

Mike laughed. "You're telling me that she told you that she was going to come back eight years ago to rip your throat out because she could be an animal, and you're still worried she'll do it?" Neva nodded and glared at him. "Yeah, I can see where I'd be worried, too. A woman threatens you almost a decade ago and you're still concerned she's going to make good on it after all this time. And you want her back in the bosom of your family, too. I think that you should really rethink your position on this before you find yourself with more than you can handle."

"We have expenses, too." Mike waited for Basil to continue, but he looked at Ellis when he stepped off the porch. "You don't want to be tangling with me, big boy. I know how to handle people like you."

"Do you?" Basil nodded, but he didn't look so sure now that Ellis was towering over him. "Here's the way this is going to work. You're going to get into that piece of shit car of yours, go to your equally piece of shit house, and leave us the fuck alone. And if you step even one toe onto this land again, I'm going to make it my business to make your life end very slowly and with a great deal of pain."

Mike watched Basil. Ellis, he knew, could and would do as he'd told him, and the man seemed to think so, too. When he took another step toward him, this time shoving him back onto his car with both hands and holding him down, Mike put his hand on his gun. Not to shoot Ellis, no, but to take down Neva should she try anything stupid, which it looked like she was going to do.

When the door opened behind them all, Mike turned. Christ, he'd been wrong about Dawn being pretty. She was fucking gorgeous. And the way she was standing there with her chin held high and her body hard with strong muscles, he wondered if she'd come to his pack to find herself a mate. Then she stood by Ellis, and he knew what everyone else seemed to already know. They were mates.

"Ellis, let him go. He's not worth it." Ellis seemed not to hear her, so Dawn put her hand on his arm. "Ellis, let him go. Please?"

His body shivered with his wolf. Mike would not have believed it had he not seen it with his own eyes, but Ellis wasn't a black wolf but a gray one, one that shimmered over his skin like he was going to come out, but only just held on. When Ellis let Basil go, he pulled Dawn into his arms and held her to him, protecting her with his body as Basil stood up.

"I want you to let me look here for my niece. She's here and I know it." Mike looked at Ellis, then back at Basil. "You all know that she's here, and I demand that you let me look so I can take her home with us."

Dawn started laughing first. Then Ellis. It wasn't long before the rest of them were laughing as well. Cash came down off the porch finally and patted him on the back, just laughing as hard as he was. The man was a moron. Basil Combs was a complete and utter moron.

Mike thought they were going to tell him, but no one did. When Dawn turned and looked at him, he could see that she was thrilled to know that Basil had no idea who she was. But she was afraid as well. Ellis looked at him, and he knew right then and there that whatever this man was going to say was going to be epic.

"Sheriff, if you'd be so kind as to escort this piece of shit off this land, I'd appreciate it. And I'm sure you can find it in your heart to make sure that he's aware of the charges that are being brought against him." Basil started to scream about his rights again, but Mike nodded and pulled out his gun. He'd had enough for one day.

"Get in that car and leave now before I shoot you for being a pain in my ass." Basil started to speak again, and Mike fired in the ground at his feet. "I've surely had enough of you today, buddy. Either leave now or so help me, I'm going to feed you to my pack."

After they left, with Andy and Billy following them to make sure they did, Mike sat on the porch and looked around. How the hell they'd found this place was beyond him. Addie sat beside him, and he looked over at her, just noticing that Ellis and Dawn were gone.

"They're mates." He told her he'd figured that out. "She's terrified of them. Do you want to know why?"

"I'm not sure. I want to, but I've got a feeling that it's pretty horrific." She touched his arm, and everything flooded his head. When she removed her hand, he lay back on the porch and let the information settle over him. "Christ almighty, they need to be shot or worse."

"Worse works for me." She stood up, and he did as well. "You know what Ellis is, don't you? You know just how strong he is and what he's capable of?"

"He's an alpha in his own right." Addie nodded. "Is he going to take my pack? I'd almost give it to him just so I can only be sheriff."

"He'd do a good job. But he won't take it from you." Mike nodded, almost relieved at that. "He won't kill you, but he will hurt you eventually. Not that he'll want to, but it will come to that. Pack will demand it of him. First blood, you know. That's how it can only work."

"Blood for pack." She nodded. "I don't want to die, Addie. I love my family, and I don't know...I can't be without them. I'm not...I've not been happy as alpha for a while now. I'd rather...to be honest, the minute I realized what he was, I nearly bowed before him and pledged. Not a good thing to do right then, but it was hard not to do it. Does he have any idea?"

"No. And neither does she. But I think that she's been alpha-bitch to a few of your pack already. They've been…look around, Mike, and tell me what you see." He did as she told him and didn't see anything at first. Then he saw them. There were seven or so of his own pack just on the border of the land that separated hers from the pack land. "They would have killed even you had you tried to harm her."

He knew it too. When they disappeared into the dark woods, he turned to Addie. She was smiling at him in a way that made him think of a cat that had just eaten all the cream and knew where there was a good deal more of it.

"You know what? I am almost as afraid of you as I am them." She laughed. "I like you, Addie. Always have, but if you want me to help you, I'm going to need something from you."

"You have it." He didn't tell her what it was, but he had a feeling she knew already. "And a bonus if you make it look good."

"Look good? I'll be lucky if he doesn't hand me my ass." She grinned again. "On a different note, because you're scaring the big alpha here, what happens now? With the Combs? Because you know as well as I do that they're never going to give up."

"Oh, I hope they don't. Because this is going to be fun from now on. Starting with the house they live in. Back taxes are a thing you don't want to fuck around with." He nodded. "You should call off sick tomorrow, Mike. It might be a good day to go to the pond at the back of my property. There's no signal back there, and I'm pretty sure that you'll make a good day of it if you take your son with you."

Mike got in his car and decided that he might just do that. Little Mike had been asking him for weeks now if they could do something together, and this might just be the ticket. Addie told him just as he was leaving the grounds that the boat would be there for them to use as well. And to have a good time. Mike smiled. Yep, having her on his side was a damned sight better than having her as an enemy. Any day.

~~~

Ellis lifted her body to his. He had to have her. Had to mark her now. When she wrapped her legs around his waist, it was all he could do not to take her right then and there, but he wanted her upstairs, in a bed, not in the living room where anyone could see them.

"Hurry." He growled at her, and she laughed. "I need you. Right now, and you're taking too long."

Ellis pressed her against the wall and rocked into her as he ripped her blouse open. Taking her breast into his mouth, he bit down hard and nearly came when she cried out. He wasn't going to make it to a bed if she kept this up.

The bed was right there when he entered the room. He turned to shut the door and was trying to figure out the lock when she tore his shirt from his body. Her mouth was everywhere, and not long enough for him to really enjoy it. Lifting her higher so that he could get to her jeans, Ellis ripped them off her and then stood her against the wall.

"I'm going to eat you first. I have to or you're going to hurt when I take you." Ellis dropped to his knees and tore the rest of her pants off as well as her panties. Her scent nearly made him stand up and take her then.

Her pussy was wet, dripping wet when he licked her soft folds. Spreading her open, he flicked his tongue over her hard nubbin and heard her cry out. Taking it into his mouth, he sucked on it hard at the same time he entered her

KATHI S. BARTON

with his fingers. Christ, she was soaking his hand and he'd only just started.

She rode his mouth with hard, fast strokes. He brought her twice while she held his head to her pussy, and he drank from her. When he brought her the third time, his wolf nearly took him when she came again. Ellis leaned back and let his wolf have him.

He licked her from gate to clit. Dawn cried out with her climax again, and when his wolf licked a path on her inner thigh, she spread her legs wider for him and told him to do it. His wolf lunged at her, biting deeply into her flesh, and she cried out with the pain. Ellis told her that he loved her and would forever.

"Take me." He told her he wanted her, and his wolf let him go when he'd sealed her wounds. Taking Dawn to the floor, the bed just too far away, he stood up and pulled his pants off, rags now, in one swift motion.

"I'm going to hurt you." She nodded and cupped her breast while he watched her. "Christ, I thought eating you would calm me, but it's only made me want you more."

"Please, Ellis. I need you to mark me. Take me." He got back on the floor with her and thought about coming on her this way, just to take the edge off, but she opened her thighs again, and he could see how wet she was, how ready.

He fisted his cock as he slowly entered her. He moaned when she seemed to pull him inside of her, and nearly slammed forward when she cried out again. Rubbing his cock over her clit, he leaned over her and suckled at her breasts. And when she came the next time, Ellis filled her.

Her scream made him stiffen as he stilled, but she pulled him closer even in her pain. Ellis wanted to take her over and over, but knew that she was hurting. Lifting his head, he looked down at her tear-stained face and wiped the tears with his thumb.

"You're very large." He nodded, and her body shifted beneath him. "I love the way you feel on top of me."

"You're very beautiful right now. Not that you weren't before, but I love you naked with my cock inside of you." She moved again, and he groaned. "Unless you want me to come inside of you right now, I'd suggest that you be still."

"You mean you don't want me to do this?" Her body moved again, and he rocked into her. "Yes. Do that again. I love that."

He moved slowly, filling her then pulling out. His body ached to empty inside of her, fill her with his seed as he marked her. But he watched her face. When she wrapped her legs over his legs, he moved harder, faster into her until she was moving with him. When she came this time, her body milking his cock, Ellis offered her his throat, and she took him hard.

Ellis came hard, emptying not just his balls into her but his heart as well. He loved her. She was his. And when she sealed the wounds at his throat, he fucked her again until she came, and then marked her with his own bite. Ellis had a mate. And he loved her very much.

CHAPTER 5

Addie handed over all the paperwork she had to him, and Ellis just stared at it. He had no more idea what to do with it than he would if someone had handed him a lab coat and told him to cure cancer. When he tried to give it back to her, she smiled.

"Shawn and Mike are going to take care of it. And Dawn asked me about a policy the other day, something that her aunt said she was no longer getting. It's from her mother. She set it up while she was in prison. And someone has been paying the premium since she died a few years ago." Ellis asked her who, and she said she didn't know. "I have been putting out some feelers on her dad. I'm assuming that he was a shifter or Dawn wouldn't be. Anyway, nothing as yet."

Ellis looked up at the stairs. Dawn was still asleep, and he thought maybe she needed to be here to hear this information. But he didn't want her upset over anything right now, and she needed the sleep. He looked at Jarrett when he laughed.

"You're in love with her." He told him he was. "Good. It looks very good on you. And, so you know, Dan is doing a fantastic job on the library. He told me to tell you that he'd have it done tomorrow if you managed to stay away another day or two."

"We should have this place done tomorrow, too. Not the roofing yet; the shingles are behind schedule a little, but the rest will be done." He got up and paced the large kitchen they were in. "They didn't know who she was. Not even to stare to try and see if it was her."

"I saw that, too. It's a good thing. If they come here, it means she'll be safe if you're not around." He shook his head at Jarrett. "I know you won't leave her, but something might happen that takes you away from her. And she is a pretty strong shifter."

"She's terrified of them." He pulled a glass from the cabinet and offered them each one as well. As he poured three glasses of tea, he continued. "I don't blame her. I know a little of what they did to her, and how they kept her locked up like they did for so long."

"It was verbal, too." Ellis looked at Dawn when she entered the room and gave her his glass of tea. "Thank you. I've never been able to get over the fact that they hated me so much. If they didn't want me, then they shouldn't have taken me in."

"It was the money." Ellis asked Jarrett what money. "Mostly it was the federal money they got. Food stamps, a check to care for you. Then there was the allotment they got from the government on other things. I think that's why Basil decided to quit his job. Everywhere they said that they had to take you—piano lessons, games, and practice for sports you were in—they got money for that too."

"I didn't go to any of those." Ellis watched her face as it came to her what the hell was going on. "Oh my God. They lied to everyone, not just me."

"Pretty much. But today we're going to have some fun with them. Shawn is going over with Mike today to serve them. Addie is suing them. Basically, while they own the property they live on, they haven't paid taxes in years. Not to mention, when they bought the property a few generations ago, they were to maintain it and to keep it looking neat. It was part of the deal that Addie's great-grandmother made with their relatives."

"Will it kick them off the property?" Addie told her that they'd have ninety days to comply. "They won't be able to do that. The place...have you seen it? I think there are cars in the yard under some of that grass, and then there are the bags of trash in the back. I've gone over there a couple of times recently just to check to see if they're still alive."

Jarrett stood up and put his glass in the sink before speaking. "If I were you, I'd try to be hanging around the area at about two today. Could be fun."

CHAPTER 6

Dawn landed on the limb above Ellis. He'd left a few minutes before her because she'd been in the middle of putting a roast in the oven when he'd told her he needed to go. She was nervous but knew that if anything happened, it wasn't going to be to her. When she looked down at him he was looking up, and she moved to the ground next to him and shifted into her wolf.

You're a beautiful wolf. Has anyone ever told you that? She moved closer to him until their bodies were touching. *I want more than anything to run with you when this is over. Do you think you could do that?*

I'd like that. They looked up when a car pulled into the driveway. It was just before two, and she watched as her aunt and uncle came out onto the porch. Her uncle had a gun in his hand. *Do you think they see that?*

I just told Mike it was there. He said he had his eye on it. You notice that he's got his ready as well. Nothing is going to go down that they're not ready for. They both slid a little closer when Shawn started talking.

"Mr. Basil Combs, my name is Shawn Connor. I'm here to represent Mrs. Addison Emerson. This is—"

"You get your hinny butt back in your car and get off my land. I've had enough of you peoples to last me a long time. Like you done told me over there, this here is called trespassing." The gun didn't move, but Mike stepped a little closer and a little bit in front of Shawn. "You ain't got no cause to come here and harass me. I done nothing wrong."

"You're in violation of the contract you have with Mrs. Emerson. The land and the property was to be kept in a neat and orderly fashion, lawn to be maintained, as well as—"

"I got me no help around here. And if you think I can afford to hire me out some people to do the work, then you're dumber than that man in the place over." Basil huffed. "Did you know he went and put up a gate in concrete? How the heck do I get on there to look around if he don't take that down? I can't. We tried for nearly an hour to get that thing out of the ground."

"You're not supposed to be able to get in, you dumb fuck." Mike looked like he was going to pull his gun and shoot her uncle anyway. "They told you yesterday that it was private property and you need to stay off their land."

"Well, I'm telling you the same thing today. Get off my land. This here is private property." He laughed then, and Dawn felt her skin crawl. She knew that laugh. "I'd really hate to have to kill you both and have to explain why I did it. You're trespassing, plain and simple like."

"You lift that gun up more than it is right now, Combs, and I will tear you apart before you can get the trigger pulled."

Dawn felt the low growl run through Ellis. When he stood up she did as well, but she moved back out of his way. He was furious looking, and she wasn't going to be hurt when he had to help Mike. And she had no doubt that Mike was going to need it.

"I don't want you here. So you get your butts on out of here." There was anger in her uncle's voice, as well as something she couldn't figure out. Then it occurred to her that he was afraid of them.

"This is telling you that you have ninety days to clean this place up or the Emersons will come in and take it from you. They are well within their rights as the original property owners." Basil actually pulled out his cock and pissed on the papers that Shawn had laid on the porch for him. "Nice job there. But it does not negate the fact that you've been served. Everything that we're doing now is being recorded. You might want to wave at the camera."

It was almost funny, seeing her uncle put his dick away quickly and catch himself in his zipper. Mike laughed out loud and asked him if he needed a minute. The cursing that came from her uncle made her blush. Who knew he knew that many bad words?

"I'm not gonna do anything around here, because I just don't want to. You want it cleaned up so bad, you do it yourself." Shawn nodded, then looked at Mike. He had his gun out now, resting by his leg. And Ellis didn't look like he'd relaxed either.

"You've been served, and you have three months to get this under control."

Shawn turned his back on her uncle, and in that split second she saw Ellis leap. Shawn was down, his body covered by Ellis, when the shots were fired. Dawn had shifted and took to the skies to keep from getting hurt herself. When she landed, it was to see what had happened.

Her uncle was lying on the porch, holding his leg and screaming like he was dying. Her aunt was trying to wrestle the gun from him to more than likely shoot Mike, who was holding his gun on Aunt Neva and Uncle Basil. Shawn was just lying there, and she just knew he'd been killed.

He's not dead. Unconscious, but not dead. I think I knocked him into the car when I took him down. Where are you? She told him and saw him look at her. *You're okay then? I saw you shift, and I was so glad to see you go to someplace safe.*

You think that Mike will arrest him now? Ellis told her he hoped so. *Stupid man. What the fuck was he thinking, pulling a gun on a cop?*

He's a moron. Dawn laughed and was glad to hear Ellis do the same. *You're really okay then? You didn't get hurt at all?*

No, I'm fine, really.

She watched as Mike came up on the porch and demanded the gun. Aunt Neva screamed at her uncle not to give it to Mike, but he did. And when he had it, he put cuffs on Uncle Basil while Aunt Neva called him every name she could string together.

About ten minutes later an ambulance showed up, as well as Addie and Jarrett. As they passed by the cruiser where Shawn was, Jarrett tossed a bag at his brother Ellis. It had never occurred to her that he was naked when he shifted. Her body warmed up at the thought.

Behave yourself. I'm going to have to finish up here before we can have that run. She told him that she was ready now. *But I have to see to this. Jarrett and Addie need to be made aware of what is going on, and I want to make sure that your relatives are put somewhere safe from harming others. He really is an idiot. You know that, don't you?*

I know. She watched as he was looked over, along with Shawn. He had a nice bump on his head, but he told them he was fine. It could have been a good deal worse. Her uncle had only a minor flesh wound. The bullet had only grazed his thigh, which would need stitches, but he was facing jail time. Dawn told Ellis she was going home, and to let her know when he was ready to leave there to run.

The house was her haven. She knew that she could and should get out more, but the thought of going into town scared her too much. She did need to go in sometime soon to get more supplies and a few things at the grocery, but she'd been putting it off. After she changed into her jeans and an old tee-shirt, she found Andy and Billy in her kitchen. Andy flushed when she startled them.

"Sorry, miss, but we was just getting us something to snack on." She eyed the five sandwiches on his plate and that many on Billy's plate. "We're gonna eat you out of house and home, I'm thinking."

"You might." She asked them if they wanted anything to drink and handed them three bottles of water each as she continued. "I have to go into town today to replenish my supplies. How much longer are you guys going to be here?"

"Shingles just got here, so we can put them on today. Then we're done with our part. Going back with Miss Addie and Mr. Jarrett when they go, I think." Dawn felt a wave of sadness wash over her at them leaving her. "Mr. Cash is going back, too, I'm thinking. He's got himself some ideas now on some of the things you use in your own garden. Miss Sloan, you should see her garden. It's really nice. Big as yours, too."

"He helped me on a few things, too." Which he had. Planting seedlings in half egg shells was brilliant. The shell would provide a nice start for the seed and give it a little extra when it was growing. "And he got mine all plowed up nice and neat for me as well. I think I might miss you guys."

Billy grinned around his sandwich but waited until he swallowed before he spoke. "We're gonna miss you, too. You don't care none when we goof off a little in the lake out back. And the fishing is great. Me and Andy was gonna go and plop our hook in it today before we go just to fill up your freezer a little more for you." She nodded. "I sure did love that trout you made last night. Man, that was some good fish."

She nodded at them both and started to put things away. They would do it, she knew, but she was really embarrassed and had to do something. When Ellis told her he was leaving the house now, she told him that the boys were going fishing.

Good, that will keep them out of trouble while I chase you down.

Her body warmed up again, and she looked out the window of her kitchen. Going out into the yard, she told Andy and Billy to have fun and left them to their own devices. She had no idea where Cash was, but assumed he was safe and more than likely flirting with some woman in town. He was really good at that.

Ellis spoke to her again. *I'd like for you to run with me.* Dawn told him she'd like that too. *I want you naked when I get to the big tree next to the pump. Do you know where that is?*

Yes. But I thought we were going to run together. He told her that he wanted to run her down and then fuck her. *Oh yes. I'd like that as well.*

Taking off her clothing, she felt a little exposed. But when Ellis came out from a stand of trees she stopped trying to hide herself and stood so he could see as much as he wanted. When his wolf came to her and sniffed at her pussy, she let him, knowing that he was getting her scent.

Christ, he loves you. So do I. Dawn moaned when he licked her cream off her thigh. *Run for us. Run and let us catch you.*

As soon as she took off, Dawn was glad that she'd left her shoes on. The ground was covered in broken branches and twigs, so running barefooted would have been painful. Leaping over a fallen log, she felt his wolf hit her from behind and she tumbled over and over until he was atop her. Laying there panting, she ran her fingers through his fur until he hummed softly at her.

Shift for me. She let her wolf take her, and felt her feet tangle in her shoes. When they were off, she rolled to her belly and tried to get out from under Ellis. *Christ, he's not going to let you go now.*

At first she was excited, her body on fire for his wolf, but when he bit her, sank his sharp canines into her shoulder, she tried to get away harder. But the more she struggled, the harder he bit her. When he mounted her, his cock filling her from behind, her wolf snarled at him, then tried to buck him off. But he was bigger and held her down while he took her.

The wolf came fast. He roared out his own release even as Dawn felt decidedly unfulfilled. Ellis told her to shift back, and before she knew what he was going to do, his cock filled her pussy and he fucked her harder than the wolf had.

"Come for me." She cried out when he lifted her ass up and pounded her harder. When his mouth moved to her breast, Dawn cupped it for him and held it to his mouth while he suckled first one then the other. She was so close, ready to come with him, when he bit her hard enough to draw blood. It was all it took to not just take her over the edge, but to drop kick her hard and let her freefall. Dawn came three more times, one right after the other, before he threw back his head and cried out his own release.

As he dropped onto her, she giggled. His head lifting up from her breast made her think he didn't think this was funny. That, of course, made her laugh all the harder. He had to ask her twice what she was laughing about.

"You. Your wolf is very selfish with satisfying his mate, but you nearly kill me with making sure I have all the pleasure I can handle and then some." He kissed her on the mouth as he laid his head on her breast again. "I love you, Ellis. And I'm going to miss you."

He raised his head and looked confused. "Miss me? Are you going somewhere? I hope not. I kinda like it here for now. And I have to finish the interior work on the bedroom."

"Aren't you going back with the rest of them?" He shook his head, even more confused. "I thought you have a business to run there. Jarrett said you own a construction company."

"I do. But you're here and that's where I'm going to be. I'll have to go in sometimes to see about jobs and such, but until you're ready to move with me, I'll be here with you." She touched her hand to his face. "I can't leave you, Dawn. I just found you. And I need you to feel comfortable with moving with me. Or not. We can just as easily stay here. I have a house that's under construction that I'd like...it doesn't matter. If you want to stay here, then we do."

"You have a house?" He told her yes as he lay back on her breast. She jerked his head up by his hair and growled at him. "What kind of house do you have? A bachelor pad, no doubt."

"No, it's a log cabin. A big one, of course, but it's all hand-hewn logs. Five bedrooms and six baths. I wanted to have a house when I met my mate so we could start having a family right away." He wiggled his brows at her. "We could keep practicing on that part if you want."

"You're building a log cabin?" He nodded and smiled. "A huge log cabin where? In the woods? Is there room for a garden? Can we...will we have neighbors?"

"Yes, it's in the woods. Deep on the property of about five hundred acres. A garden? I don't have one yet, but there's room for one. And no, there aren't any neighbors for a few miles. I like it quiet too." He rolled to his back, taking her with him. "All I have up right now is the walls. And while I've been up here, the roof was put on. I wanted to be there for that part, but it's better that I wasn't."

"Why?" He was stroking his fingers down her back, and she yawned before continuing to pepper him with questions. "I would have thought you'd want to be there for the entire thing."

"I had to be here. I needed to meet you." He yawned too. "Then there is the fact that Dan, my foreman, said he worked better when I was gone. I've been in a shitty mood of late."

"You need to go back and see to your house, Ellis. I feel bad that you're not there for it." She yawned again and closed her eyes. "I need just a few minutes of a nap, and then I have to get back to the house. Andy and Billy are going to fill my freezer, they said, with fresh fish, and I want to make sure they realize that they have to be cleaned and gutted first before they stick them in there still flopping around."

Ellis laughed a little, and Dawn smiled. This was nice, just being here and relaxed. When she yawned again, she let sleep take her under, feeling safe and protected for the first time in her entire life.

~~~

Ellis woke when someone touched his mind. He lay still, not wanting to wake Dawn just yet and not sure if there wasn't someone close to him. When he opened his eyes, Hunter spoke to him with humor in his voice.

Andy thinks that you're dead. He and Billy have been back at the house for over an hour waiting for you, and think that someone has killed you. I assured them that you were well and that I'd send you home. Hunter laughed again. *They're actually more concerned with Dawn than you, but I didn't want you to be pissy.*

She's here with me. Ellis took a deep breath and let it out slowly, marveling at how wonderfully clean it smelled here. *We're going to stay here for a while. I like it here and she's happy here. It's not that far if someone wanted to come and see us.*

I'll talk to Sloan. She said something about the charity thing today, and I really wanted to see if you were going to bring Dawn with you. He'd forgotten about it and told Hunter. *Yeah, I thought so. It's this Saturday. You have less than a week to convince her to come here and get a dress for this thing. Your tux is already here. I put it in the room you're staying in.*

How's the house...my house? The roof on? Hunter laughed. *Oh no, please tell me that it's not fallen down around my ears before I get to live in it?*

No. It's fine. And so you know, should you want to sell, Graham is interested. He said that it's perfectly situated on the waterways that he works in. Ellis didn't tell him no. He really liked it here better than anyplace he'd been. And he'd thought of the perfect place to build a house should they stay. He'd have to talk to Addie about the property. *Anyway, the roof is on and some of the interior walls are up too. The second floor is laid, and good job on the slate there. Sloan wants to do that in the dining room this summer.*

It was cheap and sturdy for that area. Tell her I know where she can get a great deal on it. Hunter said he'd tell her. *What if I stayed here? With Dawn I mean. Would you be pissed?*

No. So long as you're happy and settled, I don't care. And it's not like it's that far. Seven hours by car, and only an hour or so by plane. Just far enough, as far as Ellis was concerned. *What about the company? Would you sell out?*

No. I can run it from here too. Keep it in my name. It's not like I have to watch over the crew I have anyway. Dan does a good job. And maybe if I make him partner, he'll not be my competition too. Hunter told him that was a good idea. *So you're okay with this then? If I stay up here and belong to another pack?*

I think you should consider running your own pack. Ellis started to tell him that wasn't in the cards for him, but Hunter cut him off. *Listen to me. Mike wants out. He told me as much the last time I was up there. His little boy misses him now that he's the sheriff, and he'd love being able to go home at night after the day job and spend it with him and his wife. They're expecting their next child in a few weeks.*

I know nothing about running a pack. I don't even know if I'm the right kind of wolf to be taking over either. Hunter laughed. *What the fuck is so funny?*

You are. You're running the men you have up there now. And so is Dawn. Did you know that she made Andy promise that he'll finish college? Also that Billy gets his own place, that he's too old to be living at home? She was gentle about it, I guess, but they're already thinking she's their alpha-bitch.

Ellis thought about it but didn't agree with his brother. Hunter was just talking, that was all. He was no more alpha than he was a gardener. He'd leave that to the professionals. But when Hunter reminded him again about the charity thing, he told him he'd talk to Dawn. She woke a few minutes later, stretching over him like a large, warm cat.

"We have to go back to my home Wednesday. It's Monday now, so that should be enough time, don't you think?" She shook her head, and he could see her fear. "Let me start over. I have to go home by Friday. There's this huge event that Addie is in charge of. A charity event that raises money for abused children and adults. She wants us all to be there."

"I know. I donate to it every year. But I don't have to go with you." She stood up and reached for the clothing that she'd brought out with her. He'd never even noticed it until just then. "You have to go, but I don't."

"Then I won't go." She looked ready to argue. "I'm not going if you don't go with me. I don't really care if I go or not, but to have you on my arm would be great. Of course, I'm going to make you explain it to Sloan and Addie. They're in charge of it this year. And so is Jack. She's in charge of seating this time, so you'll have to tell her how you messed up her seating arrangements. Then there's—"

"I'm not going." He nodded and stood up, reaching for his own clothing. "I'm serious, Ellis. I'm not going. I have things to do here, and I don't do well with people. Plus, what would I wear? What would you wear?"

"I have a tux. Got fitted for it and everything. All of us Emerson men have them now." He grinned at her. "Dad will be disappointed, too. I think he was supposed to sit to your right. He'll not have anyone to dance with but Hunter."

"I'm not going." He nodded again. "I mean it. Don't even try to talk me into it. I'm not ready to go out to that kind of event, if I ever will be."

She kept telling him that all the way back to the house.

CHAPTER 7

"You have to get me out of here. Go to the bank and tell them they have to give you the money." Basil was scared to be in jail. He'd been okay in the hospital, but when he was fit to move, instead of taking him home with a pretty nurse to care for him, they'd taken him to jail and had one of the men there take care of his wound. And Neva was being no help whatsoever.

"And what do you think I should tell them, Basil? My husband shot at a cop and a lawyer, and now he wants me to bail his butt out of jail so he can come home and help me clean up the yard before them yahoos throw us off our land? He'll laugh at me." She pouted her lips at him, and he felt his heart melt for her. He loved his Neva more than he did anything else. "And there ain't no more money coming in either. That last check we got from that social services place is no good. The bank took it and told me that I was done receiving them, too."

"Darn it all to heck. They told us as long as we was caring for her, we'd get the check. Did they tell you why?" She nodded and wiped at a tear. "Don't be crying, honey.

You know that just tears me up inside. What did they say to you that's got you all dewy?"

"They know she's not there no more." He leaned back on his bunk and stared at her as she continued. "That man told them that she's been gone from our house for over eight years. Is that right, Basie? Has she been gone that long?"

"I guess." He asked her which man she was talking about, the sheriff or the lawyer. "That guy in the suit that you peed on his papers. That was funny, you know. You peeing on those things. I wish you'd have killed them though. We'd not be in this if you had."

"I can't no more kill someone than you could, not no more." She nodded, and he leaned his head on the wall behind him. "We have to get her back. I know if we can prove she needs our help, we can get all that back, including her insurance money. That sure was helpful to us all that time."

Neva was shaking her head. "They said we have to pay that all back, too. All of the social service money and the insurance money. That man I talked to said we was fraudulentmental on that." He told her fraudulent, and she nodded. "So because she's been gone all this time and they can prove it, we have to give it all back. We don't have that money no more, Bassie. We used it all up."

"We did. But it was ours in having to take her in with us."

He'd never liked Dawn. Not even her mother for that matter. She'd been a bad person when they were kids, and then when she'd been caught with her pants down and a baby in her belly, she'd told him she'd found her a love of her life. And then she was in prison for something. Good riddance to her and her brat.

Her being in prison when she'd died only told him he'd been right about her all this time. It didn't matter to him that she tried to tell him that she'd changed, gotten religion while she'd been in jail. And no matter how many times she'd begged him to bring her the brat of a daughter, he'd never done that either. It wasn't safe for her to be away from the house.

Basil had gone to see her mother once or twice while she'd been in prison, just to see if she had any more money for them. When she'd told him all her money was going for a policy for her daughter, he'd sneered at her and told her that her kid was dead. He knew it was wrong of him, but at that point, he'd not been getting any checks from the government and he was still working. Someone at the jail had told him how to get some financial help. Who knew that the less you worked the more you could get for taking in someone else's kid?

"We're gonna have to find her anyway. She's more than likely got some stash somewheres that she can give us. We did take her in when we didn't have to." Neva nodded. "You know that man and woman at the house down the road? I'm betting they know where she is. They had a look on them like they knew everything. Go on down there and have a talk with them."

"They done made it so you can't get in the drive, remember? And I don't have no more money for gas anyway." He wanted to scream out his frustrations, but didn't want to upset his Neva. "I brought in some of our cans we'd been saving. I'm planning on going by the recycle place to get me some of that. I think I got me enough to get back home with."

"You're so smart, honey. I never would have thought of that. You might be able to bring them all in and get enough to pay my bail, too. Sweet talk that guy at the place so you can get him to put a little extra in the envelope like you did the last time." She'd put her foot on the scale and had upped the weight by about fifteen pounds. "You're such a wonderful wife. I don't know what I'd do without you."

After she left telling him she'd take care of him, he was brought his meal. He didn't want to eat it, but the last time he'd refused to do that, they'd just taken it away and told him to starve. He thought he might have if he'd not been begging for a drink and was brought a cola. Goodness gracious, these men were hard and mean to him.

As he picked up his plastic fork and knife, Basil began to cut into the hard crusty meat. He thought it was chicken, but wasn't entirely sure. When cutting it proved to be too hard, he opened his stale bun and put it there. He was still chewing his first bite when a man pulled a chair up in front of his cell.

"Mr. Basil Combs?" Basil nodded but couldn't speak around the lump of food in his mouth. "I'm here from the state department of taxation. I'm here to ask you about some unpaid taxes on the property you're living on."

"I don't work, so I don't have to pay any taxes." The man only nodded. "No. I get me a nice refund every year, but I don't ever have to pay any. It's a nice big check, too. Head of household and all. You got me a refund? I sure could use it about now."

"No. And if you own property, you shouldn't be getting the refunds you've been receiving. But property tax, which this is, has nothing to do with your federal income." Basil had taken another bite of his sandwich as the man continued. "You owe for the past twenty-seven years. Nothing has been paid on it since it was transferred to your name. You owe a great deal with penalties."

"I ain't got no money, and I'm not paying no property taxes either. I just told you, I don't work." The man pushed a file at him, and Basil took it without thinking. "I don't care what this here thing says, I'm not paying 'cause I don't have a job."

The man stood up. "Then perhaps you should think about finding one, because as of right now, you have thirty days to come up with the funds to pay the taxes on the land or we're going to take it from you." Basil opened the file and looked at the staggering amount. "Have a good day, sir."

"A good day? How the heck do I have a good day when you're taking my land? And that other person, that other woman says I have to clean it up or she'll take it. You darned people are messing things up for me. I don't have a job." He was still shouting when the officer who had brought him his meal came into the long hall. "Did you see this? He wants me to come up with over two hundred thousand dollars in thirty days. I don't even got me a job that'll pay for my bail to get my person out of here."

"Sucks to be you, I guess." The officer reached for his tray, and Basil took off the apple and the cola that were still left on it. He had to give up the pie, which he supposed was good because he was still tasting that one from yesterday. Darn, but he'd not had a good meal since that brat had left them.

"And for what reason?" He finished his sandwich and started on the apple. It was hardly fit to be called that, but it would be hours before he was given anything else. "Sure, we tied her up, but that was to keep us safe. She might have gotten it into her head to tear into us or something."

Basil had seen shifting people before. There were a couple of wolves that had been on his land once that he'd fired at. Not killing them or anything, but he'd made sure they knew that they weren't welcome. But when Dawn had her one of them shifts, he'd been a little afraid of her. It was not like they were bad to her, but she might not see it the way he and his Neva had.

If things didn't look up soon, he and his wife were gonna be living in the house without a means to get to their car. He was pretty sure they'd make it so he'd not be able to park his car on the land when they took it. What was he supposed to do with it then? Opening the cola, he took a long sip of it while he tried to work it out.

He really did wonder how he was going to manage living in the house if the land belonged to someone else. There had to be some provisions so that he could get out of the place to go to town when he needed to do some shopping. Surely, they didn't think he was going to fly to it, did they? If anyone else came to see him, he'd ask. They'd be able to tell him how he was going to work that.

Dozing just a little, he was startled awake by that lawyer person, Shawnee or something like that. The man told him his name again, and Basil nodded, wondering what the heck else could go wrong today. Then he remembered his question and asked him.

Shawn's blank stare made Basil think that he didn't know either. Basil was quite proud of himself for coming up with something that would stump a suit. But before he could crow about it too much, rub it in his face, the man threw back his head and laughed. It was a good five minutes before he got some control over himself to answer him.

"The land and the property are one thing. Anything you have on the property is considered a part of it. The house, the cars, even any sheds or outbuildings you have on the land will belong to my client."

Basil told him about the tax man. "I tried to tell him that I don't have to pay them when they're giving me money not to have a job. But he just kept telling me that I gotta pay them. Two hundred thousand dollars' worth of that shit. I did never get that much in refunds." Shawn told him he'd more than likely have to pay that back as well. "Why for?"

"Did you claim that you had property to get those refunds? Tell whoever did your taxes for you that you owned land?" He told him his wife did them for them. "Then she should have known better than to not claim the land as income too."

"The land don't pay me nothing. How the hell is that considered income?" Basil shook his head. "I think you all are making this crap up as you go."

"It's property and, as such, considered income." Shawn shook his head again as he laughed. "You really do think that this is just going to go away, don't you?"

"I just think I'm being hosed, and I'm a good guy." Shawn handed him a file, and he was almost afraid to open this one. Instead, he put it on the bed next to him. "Just tell me what it says. I got enough surprises for one day."

"That says that you'll leave the premises post haste and never return." Basil tried to wrap his mind around what he was saying, and Shawn sighed heavily before he could ask him what the heck he'd just said. "You'll leave the house and the property as soon as you're released from jail and never return."

"I ain't gonna do that. I got stuff there. That place has been in my family for a long time. What if my kids want it?" Shawn asked him if he had any. "Well, no, but that don't mean we might not have some one day. Me and Neva just ain't in a position to bring them into the world just yet."

Basil thought he said thank God but wasn't really sure. When he spoke again, Basil listened, but all he could think about was having a baby with his Neva. Basil interrupted Shawn, not really listening anyway.

"How old you gotta be to be too old to have a kid? I mean, I got me some juices left. What about Neva?" He asked how old she was. "We're in our fifties. She's a might older than me, but she's still just as lovely as when I first met her."

"I'm pretty sure you're past the time to start a family, but you might want to check with your doctor." Nodding, Basil thought about having to find one first, but that was down the road for now. They had to get this money thing taken care of first. "About the house and land. You leave now, for good, as soon as you're released, and my client is willing to pay off the taxes and assume the responsibility of cleaning up the place."

"Well, that's right nice of them. Tell them I said thanks." Basil leaned back on the little cot and thought of how nice it would be to live with the place all cleaned up. "Any chance of us getting something for our own selves out of this? I don't mean to be greedy none, but it would be nice to have some pocket money and all."

"I'm to cut you a check for five thousand dollars as soon as you agree to the terms." Basil nodded again. "You'll leave as soon as you're released?"

"Sure. Sure. We just gotta get us a few of our things out first. When you think they'll start on the yard? It's been a long time since we've had us a mower. My niece should have been doing it, and when we get her back, we'll make sure it's all caught up. But for now, how long you thinking?"

Shawn told him to sign off on the pages where the little tabs were. He even handed him a really pretty pen to do it with. Basil thought of asking if he could keep it, but didn't. He was nice enough to pay off the tax man and clean up his yard for him. He didn't know where they'd have to stay until it was done, but he'd figure something out.

"As soon as you're out of the house, give me a call at this number. Then they'll begin working on the place. The taxes, all of them, will be paid, but you're going to be responsible for any other fines and back taxes you might owe. As for the social services money, you'll also have to take care of that." Basil nodded. "You'll be out within twenty-four hours, right?"

He told him he'd be out by then. Just as soon as he was released. Wait until Neva heard about this. She was going to be as happy as a clam. A nice clean house and a yard they could walk around in. Man, things were looking up.

~~~

"I cannot believe you talked me into this." Ellis only smiled at Dawn. "You tricked me, and here I am."

"All I said was that I wasn't going without you. You're the one that called Sloan and told her that I was being stubborn." He laughed, and she glared at him again. Something that she'd been doing for three days now. "You're going to love my family. Hunter and the rest of them are waiting at the house to see you. I didn't think you'd want them all there at once."

"I don't want to do this." It was, of course, too late, but he only held her hand. "Ellis, they're going to think you've really fucked up with this. I like your dad and all, but he's bound to have told them what kind of person I am."

"I'm sure he has. Dad loved you and he's more than likely singing your praises about how wonderful you are. And how lucky I am to have you in my life." Her fingers tightened in his hand and he kissed her. "It's going to be just fine, Dawn, you'll see. They'll love you. And after the event on Saturday, we'll come back if you want to."

"I want to now." He nodded and held her. When she looked out the window, Ellis wondered what she was going to do when she found out that the entire pack was coming for a pack meeting tonight. He hadn't told her because he was too afraid she'd back out. And Ellis wanted to show her off. Besides, she'd be fine so long as he didn't leave her. He hoped so anyway.

When they landed, there was a limo waiting for them, along with Jack, Sloan, and Addie. He'd forgotten they were going to take her shopping, and tried to think how to tell her now without having her freak out. Seeing Addie helped, but when his brother Graham pulled up in the truck to take him, she looked terrified.

"You have to have a dress. Remember?" She nodded and gripped his hand tighter. "Honey, you know Addie.

And Jack and Sloan are two of the nicest women I know. They won't hurt you."

"I know that." Her snapping at him nearly had him laughing, but he just caught himself. "I can take care of myself. But I didn't know they were going to be there too. I thought it would just be the two of us."

"I know nothing about dresses and all the mysteries that go into putting one on. I can certainly strip one off you if you have it on, but as far as the things that go with it, I'm lost." She glared again. "Christ, you're beautiful when you're pissed off. I'll be only a call away if you need me, but I don't think you will. Graham and I are going over some plans about the house, and then he said he was going to make me an offer. We'll be free to live in your little house when Addie decides on a price."

"She said she'd do it before we left." He nodded. "You don't really want to sell your house, do you? We can...we can live here if you want."

"I want you to be happy. And wherever that is, that's fine with me." She nodded and Addie and the rest of them came toward them. "Sloan is the pregnant one, and Jack is the one that looks like she'd beat you up if you talk to her funny. I love them all to death, and they'll love you."

When she got into the limo with them, he thought of the first day of school and when his mom had brought him to the class then left him. He'd felt abandoned and lonely too. But within minutes, he was making friends and forgot all about the fact that he'd not wanted to go at all. His mom had been right, as usual.

"The house is up, so to speak. The interior walls need to be put in, but Dan said that I needed to pick out where I wanted plugs and shit like that." Ellis started to point out that they'd not come to an agreement yet, but he let Graham talk. "I talked to Sloan's cook, and she's going to help me pick out the kitchen stuff. Are you sure you want to do this?"

"Honestly? Yeah, I think I do. If I can get a good price on Addie's land and you with the house, we're going to build deeper in the woods. Another log cabin. That's what she has her heart set on." Graham asked him about the rest of it. "You mean the pack? I don't think that's going to be in the cards just yet. I'm happy just being a boss. And I need to talk to Dan about a partnership as well."

"I haven't said anything, as you requested, but I think he'd go for it." They were pulling into the long drive of what would more than likely be Graham's house. "Well, here you go."

It was much bigger than he'd thought it would be. Even with the doors and windows not put in, he knew it was going to be gorgeous. He could not wait to see it finished. As Graham took him inside the place, he could see the changes that Graham had been talking about since he'd asked him if he really wanted to purchase it, such as the hardwood floor in the dining room. The slate that he'd wanted in the kitchen was there, but the cabinets that held the china were all open with lights in them. The built in cabinets in the bathrooms were a nice touch, and one that he'd try to put into his own home.

He decided that bringing Dawn here would be a good thing. She could see what she wanted in their own home and things that she didn't. He was sure she'd see things that he hadn't that were nice to her but only a job to him.

Graham took him to the back of the house, which was all one floor. Ellis had wanted that to be able to use the house when he was older and not getting around as well. But their new home would be two levels, for the children they were talking about. He was excited and sad at the same time.

Living in their own house was going to be great. This house would be wonderful for Graham because he would make it his home before he found his mate, if he found her. But the more of his brothers that found their mates, himself included, the more he thought the rest of them would as well.

As they moved through the rest of the house and into the yard beyond, he thought about what else he wanted to put into his new home. Well, the yard anyway. A garden. And a big barn so she could have her own tractor and anything else that she wanted. He wasn't really into vegetables that much, but it made her happy and that was what he wanted more than anything.

When his brother said they were going to Hunter's for beer and pizza, he thought it a great time to talk to Hunter about being an alpha. Not that he thought it would come to that, but he wanted to be aware of things before it became something he had to decide on. And Dan was going to be there as well.

CHAPTER 8

"This would look amazing on you with your coloring." Dawn took the dress that was handed to her and again looked in vain for the price tag. She had asked several times where they were and was told the same thing. What did it matter?

"You do know that I have no idea what the hell you're costing me." Sloan only snorted at her. "I need to know what I'm paying for this stuff."

"Just put it on and we'll tell you. If it looks good." Dawn jerked the robe off and started to rip the dress off the hanger to put it on. But Jack's voice over the changing booth door had her pause. "And if you tear it in your pissy mood, then I'll have to find you ten more that don't suit you to try on."

She growled. Not that it had done her any good the first few times she'd done it, but she did it again. When she pulled the dress over her head she stopped to look in the mirror. Good heavens. When Dawn heard Addie laugh, she wondered if they were making fun of her and started to pull the dress off again.

I'm not making fun. I can feel that you like this dress, and I'm looking forward to seeing it on you. Dawn turned to her right, then left in the three-way mirror. *Oh, I have to see it now. Come on out. Or wait, let me come in to see if you're all tucked in the right places.*

When Addie joined her in the large room, she watched her face. Dawn loved the dress and was hoping that Addie did as well. When she asked her to turn around, Dawn felt like one of the pretty princesses she'd seen on television when she was a little girl.

"Do you like it? It's pretty, isn't it? I'm sure it costs a fortune, but Ellis assured me that he had a lot of money. I'm not really sure what he means by a lot. I mean, I feel like I have a lot when I have a thousand dollars stashed away." Addie put her hand over her mouth, then smiled at her when she pulled it away. "I'm nervous."

"No, you're gorgeous. And Ellis has a great deal of money. Millions. He and his brothers have invested well, and Sloan has helped him and the others put their money in the right places." Dawn was still trying to wrap her mind around millions when Addie told her to turn around and let her pull her hair back. "You have such beautiful hair. No matter what you do with it, it still looks good. But with this dress, you need it up and off your neck. Show off those gorgeous shoulders and make Ellis drool."

She could almost see his face when he saw it. When her hair was pulled up and into a fancy twist, she went out to the store to show off the dress. Jack whistled better than most men she knew could, and Sloan put her hand over her heart.

"You don't like it?" Sloan nodded, then shook her head. "I'm really sorry, but I do. And I think it looks good on me."

"It does, and you do. But what I meant was you can't wear those boots, and you need your hair styled." Dawn flushed hotly. "Christ, you're going to be the bell of the ball. And there is already a lot of buzz about your donation."

"My donation? I gave the same thing last year and you said it did well." Addie nodded and looked at Sloan. So did Dawn. "They didn't want it this year, right? I told you it was a dumb thing to donate, but you said it was good and people would love it."

"They do. As a matter of fact, I wanted to talk to you about advertising." Jack plopped down on the couch that they'd been using like it was their own. "You need a logo and slogan. I've been thinking about the logo all week. I like Dawn's Preserves. But that doesn't really work because—and I didn't know this—all jellies are not preserves."

"No. They're all cooked and have pectin or gelled fruit products in them. But jellies are made with just fruit juice and other liquids, while jams and preserves are gelled with pieces of fruit in them. Sometimes I put pulp in them just for the texture." Dawn looked at Jack when she nodded and smiled. "I still have no idea why my donation is causing such a problem."

"Everyone wants it. Since we put it up for auction, I've already gotten a silent bid of five grand." Dawn sat down when Addie continued. "You have no idea what a buzz this is causing us. I mean, the woman who got it last year paid fifty-three dollars for it. And that was an amazing price. But she bragged around, and then people came to me and asked me if I had any, and Bill pulled out the jars you'd sent me last year. I had to hide the last five jars of it or it would have gotten taken from me."

"I have more." Jack kissed her on the mouth. "What on earth? Did you want some too? I have about two hundred jars of it from last year. The fruit was really good, and I even bought some…what are you doing now?"

Jack was laughing as she went to the counter and asked for a pen and paper. When she came back, she sat on the couch while Dawn went in to change back into her clothing. As soon as she came out, Jack handed her a drawing.

"It's rough, so you know, but this is what I have in mind. Dawn's is perfect, just like that. And the jars will be colored in, or I can use a picture of the actual jars."

Dawn's name was written out in the prettiest font she'd ever seen, and the trees behind her name were full of fruit that Jack said she'd fill in later. The little jars, about five of them, were lined up on a picnic table that had a basket overflowing with napkins and plates. Biscuits sat on a plate with steam coming up off them.

"I still don't understand." Jack took it from her and smiled. "You do that a lot instead of answering people. It's sort of scary."

"You should market them. I'm sure with the right store front and the perfect advertising company you can make millions. And I'm not kidding about that either. Howling, my advertising company, would do all your work for you, you being family and all, but you could, say in about six months to a year, be selling to big names all over the—"

"Hold on." Dawn pointed to the paper. "You aren't serious about this. Who would buy my stuff? I mean, it's just mashed up fruit with sugar in it. It's good, but millions of dollars' worth?"

"Honey, you have no idea what you're sitting on. I took a sample to Mabel—she owns the local diner in town. She told me that it was just like her own grandmother made. And my grannie placed an order for five dozen of each kind you make to give away as gifts next year. You're sitting on a gold mine." Addie pulled her to the couch they were all sitting on. "You can do this, Dawn. You're very good at this."

"I don't think this is a good idea." They all just stared at her. "I mean, what if I had to talk to one of them? Tell someone what was...I can't talk to people very well."

"That's where I come in." She looked at Sloan when she spoke up. "Jack can do the advertising, and I'll find you a front man. Or in this case a front woman. She'll be your spokesperson, like that dog that does it for those beans."

"You want a dog to advertise my jellies?"

Sloan told her not to be silly. Dawn was trying really hard not to look dumb, but this was too much. When Ellis touched her mind to ask her if she was all right, she told him no.

Take a deep breath and let me know what's going on. If it's the cost of a dress, I told you I have the money. She told him what they were saying to her. *Oh. Well, that's a great idea. And so you know, I think Dad might have taken about a half dozen with him when he left. It's really good stuff.*

But they're saying I could be a millionaire in no time. He laughed. *This is not funny. They're being mean, telling me this kind of stuff only to take it all away.*

Dawn, honey, if they say you'll make a million, you'll probably double that. They know their stuff. Has Jack drawn you a logo yet? She did mine for me. And the letterhead on my billings. She's that good. And Sloan knows a good investment when she sees one. If she says it'll sell, then you can bet it will. She told him it was just jelly. *And it's damned good jelly. And you're going to be happy to know that Graham made me a great offer on the house. Now all we need is property to build us one on.*

I'll talk to her now. She took a deep breath. *Ellis, this dress is so pretty. Are you sure about this? I mean, taking me to this charity event?*

More sure now than ever before. He told her to have fun, and she told him to fuck off. He laughed, and she smiled. Dawn loved him so much.

"I need a place to put this all. How about you sell me the property that the house is on now and a few extra acres?" Addie nodded. "Just like that? You're not even going to try to talk me out of it?"

"No. Why would I do that? And the house is already in your name. It has been for years. As for the extra acres, I just made a deal with the farm next to yours." Dawn felt overwhelmed and said as much to Addie. "You deserve it, Dawn. You've made it your home for so long that you should have it."

"You kept me safe for all these years. It was only because of you that I was able to survive." Addie nodded and hugged her. "I love you, Addie."

"And I you. So let's get this thing going so we can go and eat. I don't know about you guys, but I'm starved." They all agreed, and Dawn was sent to the shoe department with Sloan. Addie was making arrangements to have the dress sent to her home, and Jack was looking for underthings. For some reason, that frightened her more than going into a crowded restaurant did. Jack could be dangerous.

"I want to be an investor in your new company." Dawn started to tell her that she didn't have a company, but Sloan continued. "I do it all the time. Look for businesses that I think will make me some money, and the other person a good deal more. I was an investor in Emerson Construction for a while, but Ellis was able to buy me out. It was good for both of us."

"And if I fail?" She told her she wouldn't. "But I might. I don't know what I'm doing. I haven't the slightest clue what I might be doing. I'm not even sure that you know what you're doing if you think I can make this work."

"You know as well as I do what we're doing. And as for you not having a clue what you're doing, all that would work in your favor. You have no preconceived notions about how it should work. You just want to make your jellies. I want to help you make that dream come true. For a time. After you start showing a profit, which I think will be sooner than anyone thinks, then you can buy me out."

"You do know that this just might be a fluke and that no one will want them once they realize that they're just jelly. Jelly they can purchase anywhere for a lot less than I'd have to charge." Sloan just smiled. "That's an Emerson woman trait you pick up, isn't it? You smile instead of answering, and the other person thinks you're being nice, but what you're really doing is calculating how quickly you can slit their throat."

Sloan hugged her. "I'd never cut your throat while smiling at you, Dawn. You're too scary for that."

It wasn't a compliment. It was...Dawn wasn't sure what it was. It was fucking scary was what it was, and she was pretty sure that when Sloan laughed, she'd meant it as a joke. But Dawn didn't know that many people, and this one was beyond frightening. "I'm going to like going into business with you. You're extremely intelligent and the bravest woman I know."

"Brave? How the hell do you get that? I've been hiding on my farm for years, and the thought of going to this thing with you guys has me sweating bullets." Sloan handed her a pair of incredibly high heels. "You want me to break my neck instead of cutting my throat?"

"No. What I want is for you to look as beautiful as you are." Dawn flushed hotly. "You really don't see it, do you? The fact that your aunt and uncle didn't know who you were is because you are simply gorgeous. And Ellis? I've never seen a man so besotted in my life. He worships you."

"I love him as well." Dawn held the shoes to her breast and looked at Sloan. "If I do this, and I'm not saying I will, you'll tell me right off if it's not working for either of us. And you'll not expect me to do any kind of upfront stuff. I really don't do people well."

"Deal."

Sloan agreed too quickly. Dawn had a feeling that she'd missed something, but Jack and Addie joined them and started on the shoes and how she had to get them. When she saw the price tag of nearly five hundred dollars, she handed them to Jack and told her they were perfect. It was time for her to start thinking bigger.

~~~

"And you will still be there should I need you?" For the fourth time, Ellis told Dan that he would be there whenever he needed him. "This is not what I had in mind when I came to work with you. My plan was to learn from the best, then be your competition."

114

"Now you don't have to be." Dan shook his head. It was harder to convince him that he could do this than it had been to convince Dawn to get on the jet. "You don't have to do it. But I'm not going to be around as much. My mate has a home that we both love, and we want to live up there."

He hadn't mentioned anything about the pack to anyone but Hunter. And Hunter was going to talk to Mike and see what he wanted to do before anything was done. Ellis was still not sure he could do it, but Hunter said that he had faith in him to be the best at anything he did.

"I want to do this." Dan had said that three times now but was still backtracking a little. Less now than when he'd first asked him, but still a little nervous. "My dad...he said that you were going to do this someday. Told me that a month ago. I didn't believe him. Still don't believe that you want to do this. It makes sense, I guess. Partnership over having me as competition. Not that I'd be that much, but you get it."

"I do. And I need this to work for us. You're doing a great job, and I'll be able to help out too. Just not as much as I had been." Dan nodded, but his face looked like he was thinking hard. "Just take your time and think it over. And talk to Sloan. She said that she'd help you out as much as you want her to."

"I will have to get a loan from her. And the amount of work you're talking at your end of the country will keep us working year round." Ellis nodded. "I'll call her tomorrow. I'm...I'm going to do it. It's a more than fair price to be a partner in this company."

Dan would be making as much as he did. They'd split the profit and costs down the middle from now on. If they fucked up and went in over budget, it would cost them both. If they got a bonus, they had agreed to split that between the men and be done with it. More than anything, they both wanted this to work. And Ellis knew that it would.

Hunter came out to the deck where they had been sitting and handed him a beer. He just sat it on the table, ignoring it for now. It wasn't that he didn't enjoy a good beer with pizza, but he had to drive home later and he wanted to be alert.

"Where are you staying while you're here?" Ellis looked at Hunter and realized that he'd not made any arrangements for them to live here for the weekend. "Yeah, I thought so. Sloan just called me to tell me that you're staying here. She told Dawn that it was your idea, so you know when she is pissed at you."

"Why would she be pissed at me?" Then it occurred to him. "She told her that I didn't take care of this. Damn it. That woman is going to put me in the doghouse." He wasn't mad, but he was glad for the closeness of his family.

His dad came out when they were laughing at what he'd have to do to make it up to Dawn. He sat down and took the beer that was still cold. Ellis looked at Hunter when his dad drained the bottle before setting it on the table again. Before he could ask him what was wrong, Dad started talking.

"What the hell was I thinking? I mean...shit fire and light a match stick. I just thought it would be kinda fun for her. Then she comes up and tells me that it's a date. I never agreed to no date. I haven't been on a date in...well, more years than I want to think about." He looked at them before he shook his head. "I'll just have to tell her it's not a damned date, but an outing."

"Dad?" He looked at him. "Did you ask someone to go somewhere with you? To the charity ball?"

"I did. She was going on about how it was going to raise up all this money, and I thought, why the hell not? Just tell her you'll take her. Then she comes back and says she's excited about the date. It's not a date, damn it." He nodded, and Ellis shook his head. "It's not a date, is it, son?"

"If you asked a woman to go out with you, then yeah, I'm pretty sure that it's a date." His dad got up and started pacing back and forth, talking about how women sure did get a notion in their head. "Who did you ask out?"

"I didn't ask anyone out. I thought she'd enjoy going." Dad took a deep breath and let it out slowly. "I only wanted her to see what happened at one of these things. And with you all having your own 'dates,' I thought she'd be someone I could talk to." He'd made the word "date" sound like it was something to avoid at all costs.

"That's the very definition of a date, Dad." Dad growled at Hunter, who laughed. "I'm pretty sure if you tell her it wasn't a date but an outing, she's going to smack you in the head. I would."

"She might just hit me harder than that." He sat down. "It's Mabel. Mabel Carlyle. She's been helping out with getting the food in wholesale for this thing, and I wanted to…I don't know, return the favor. I never wanted it to be something that I'm going to have to repeat."

"Dad." Hunter laughed when he said his name. "What is wrong with Mabel? I thought you and her got along pretty good. And it's not like you have to sleep with her."

Ellis heard the whop all the way across the deck. Hunter's head snapped forward like it was on a spring, and his dad didn't look like he was satisfied with just that.

"You hold your tongue, young man, or I will take you to the shed. Of all the things to say about a nice woman like her." Dad started pacing again. "We've been alone for a long time, her and me, and if we have a little romance after our outing, then we will. And it'll be none of your damned business."

"Yes, sir." Hunter looked like he was on the verge of laughing again when he looked at him. "Ellis is going to take over Mike's pack when he moves up there with Dawn."

As far as changing the subject around so that his dad would be distracted, it was perfect. Dad looked like he'd just swallowed a whole plate of the sweetest cookies ever made, and his button looked ready to pop. With one more hit to the back of Hunter's head, he came to Ellis and hugged him tightly. Hunter was going to pay for this.

"You gonna do it, really? You'd be fine at it. I know you would. A damned sight better than this idiot behind me." Dad glared at Hunter as he continued. "Don't think I don't know what you did by throwing Ellis under the bus, boy. I'm still mad at you. What a thing to say to your own father. If your mother was alive, she'd have your ass for this." No one pointed out that had she been alive, this wouldn't have happened, but his dad was still upset.

Hunter nodded and looked like he was going to say more when his cell phone rang. Standing up, he went around the deck to answer it, and Dad sat on the chair across from Ellis. He was asking him all about it, when he was going to talk to Mike and everything, when Hunter came back around to them. He looked...depressed was the only word he could think of.

"That was Margo Hemingway...she works for Pete at the armory in town. She just said...he's passed away. She thinks it was a heart attack."

Ellis stood up and went to his dad. He knew that the two of them were close friends, and he could tell that his dad was taking it hard. When Hunter said he was going to make a few calls, Ellis and his dad sat back down. Dan left too, saying he was going to tell his own father about Pete.

They sat there for several minutes. Cash wasn't saying anything, but Ellis knew that his dad was hurting. When he looked up at him, he could see that he was fighting tears, and when he wiped at his nose with his ever present handkerchief, Ellis leaned forward.

"I'm guessing that a date ain't such a bad thing when you're as old as I am, is it?" He told him it wasn't a bad thing at any age. "Old Pete, he didn't have him no kids, you know. He only had us. Nicest man I knew at any age. I'm going to...he was a good man."

"I know. He told me once that he thought of us boys as his own. He was a wonderful man and will be missed." Dad nodded. "Margo will need some help with things. I think she was working for him since his mate passed."

"I'll see to it." He stood up, and Ellis did, too. When Dad turned to look at him, Ellis wanted to hug him again. "Have me some grandbabies, will you? Lots of them. I need them."

"We'll work on that." Dad nodded and went into the house. Ellis sat down and thought of Dawn, and wondered what she'd think of his dad's request.

CHAPTER 9

In the way of the pack, Pete's funeral was held the next afternoon. Dawn watched all the people walk by the open grave and toss in memories for him to take with him on his run in the sky. It was perhaps one of the most moving funerals she'd ever witnessed, not that she'd seen that many.

Each person who walked by the grave would either toss in an envelope or a flower. Some, most of them, put in both. The flower would die, of course, and the seeds from it would mark the grave of a wonderfully amazing man. The envelopes were for him.

"Each person is to think of a time when Pete helped them with something. Or a fond memory of him that they will remember forever." Ellis explained it to her as they dressed for the meeting. "They write it out with their own hand and then seal it in an envelope that will be sealed with their own blood, not saliva. We believe that when he gets to his great run in the sky, he'll pull them out and read them, touching the lives of the people once again by sending them a good wish or a memory of his own."

"Will people have bad memories of him? I mean, can they do that? Write it out and put it there if they didn't like him?" He thought about it for a few minutes before he told her that he supposed anything was possible. "Pete was kind to me. When we were at the airport, he was there and told me…he said I was as pretty as a speckled pup under a little red wagon. Then he told me that he thought my jelly was the best he'd ever tasted, and that it was better than his own mother's."

Ellis pulled her up from the bed where she'd been sitting and held her. The man had been so nice and now he was gone.

And it seemed that she wasn't the only one who thought so. Hunter stood up after everyone had gone by to pay their respects.

"Pete was…in a word…a pistol." Everyone laughed. "The first day here most of you know that he saved my life. Had he not taken it into his head to be shot for me, I'm sure that things at the police station would have taken a different route than they did. He was a great man and will be missed by us all."

Several other people got up to say a few words. Most of them had a funny tale to tell; some told what he'd done for them that no one had known about. Every story told Dawn of the man she'd only known briefly, and made her realize what a loss it was going to be for her to have not known him well.

As the grave was filled, each of the immediate pack members, mostly the Emerson men, putting their backs into closing it up, Dawn helped bring out the food to the tables that had been set up for the feast. And what an amazing feast it was turning out to be! Had she not known for sure that the man had passed less than twelve hours ago, she would have thought that things had been organized for months, not hours. Makeshift tables were set up in seconds, platters of foods laid out in a matter of minutes, and the drink glasses were filled while everyone sat, the elder women of the pack filling and passing things as they were needed. Dawn asked Jack, who was sitting next to her, when the women who were cooking for them would sit.

"They won't. See how they have their hands in their aprons?" She watched as the women would dig deep into their oversized pockets and then shove something to their mouths. "Mostly it's cookies or a sandwich cut up into chunks. I saw one woman have an entire turkey leg in hers, and she'd pull it out when she thought no one was looking and take a big bite out of it. A few of them have a bottle of water there, too. Not many, but a few even have some hard liquor in them. Those are some really amazing aprons if you ask me."

It was amazing to watch them now that she knew what to look for. A woman of about sixty slipped some of the biscuits that she'd made into her pocket and winked at her when she saw Dawn watching. An older woman of about eighty was walking around with a pitcher in her hand, but was drinking from it rather than pouring. Most people declined her filling their glass when she'd get around to asking them.

"You'll see all kinds of stuff you'd never see at most pack meetings. It was great of Hunter to combine this memorial service with the pack meeting that was supposed to happen next week. It'll give people time to meet you and to give you well wishes." She turned and looked at Jack again. "No one told you, did they? I'm sorry."

"What is it I'm going to be expected to do?" Jack looked at Hunter, then back at her. "Jack? What is it I'm going to have to do?"

"If it were a real meeting, you'd have to shift and run with us, but since this is sort of a combo thing, nothing much more than just introduce yourself. I think most people here know of you, but they don't know you. Understand?" She nodded, her belly starting to churn up. "Just breathe, okay? You're going to be fine. Just stand next to Ellis when the time comes, say who you are and what you do. Mention the jelly. They'll love that."

Nodding again, she started to shove her plate away. Ellis, who was seated on her other side, pushed it back. When she looked at him, he winked at her, and she wondered how many people would notice if she punched him in the balls. Ellis leaned into her ear and nipped it.

"You do that and all my plans for you later will be put on the back burner. I plan to show you some pretty amazing moves." She snorted at him. "And you need to eat. If you don't, the women will think you don't like it."

Dawn started to tell him she was nervous, but he put a piece of ham into her mouth. She had to admit, it was the best tasting ham she'd eaten in a while. When she was finished chewing it, he gave her another piece and then another. It was sort of romantic the way he was feeding her. Then she realized what he was doing. Distraction. She realized this when Hunter stood up again and the entire group got quiet.

"My brother and his new mate are here tonight. Dawn Whitfield Emerson has joined us from up north. She and Ellis have decided to build a home there. Graham is going to buy his home here, and Addie and Jarrett have sold them a nice piece of property up that way as well. They're going to be home so often, however, that we won't miss them all that much, I think." Ellis stood up when Hunter looked in their direction. Dawn felt like she was frozen to the seat. Hunter laughed, and she looked at him, thinking that murder might be something she could and would consider right now. "She's led a very sheltered life and is a little shy. But we're very glad to have her in our family, and wish the best for them both."

She stood up then and nodded as everyone congratulated them both. When someone asked her what she did, Jack poked her in the leg. She wasn't sure this was a good idea, but looked at the woman who had snagged herself some biscuits and was currently spreading her jam on them.

"I'm going to be making jellies and preserves to sell. *Dawn's* is what Jack said to call it. It's there...right here." She picked up the large bowl of it that she'd put there not an hour ago. "I made this." Before she could set it back down, Ellis took it from her and passed it to the man on his other side when he said he wanted more. Dawn laughed when he spread the apple jelly over his ham sandwich. Well, that was one way to do it.

After the meal, most everyone made their way into the dark woods. She didn't, but sat at the table that had been cleared of everything but a few glasses. Three women she had only just met and didn't really know their names sat down with her. Dawn looked around for someone to rescue her.

"I'm Martha, this is Mary, and that one over there is Claribel. Just like the big old cow." They all laughed, and

Dawn relaxed a little. "We hear tell you and Ellis are going to be pack alpha."

"I don't think so. Where did you —?" Claribel waved her off. "I think someone has given you misinformation."

"No, they didn't. I got it straight from the wolf's mouth. And you know them, they're worse than a bunch of old women around a washboard." Mary pulled a skein of yarn and a set of needles from her apron as she continued. It looked like she was knitting a baby blanket, but Dawn had no idea. "You and that Ellis, you'll make a great team up there. Teach them how we do it down here. We'll even come up for you and show you how to throw together a nice howl party."

Dawn was swept along with their story. She didn't have to say anything, and she'd already learned from them that denying it was a waste of time.

Mary continued her knitting and poking fun of anyone that caught her eye. She wasn't vicious about her observations, but it was more like she was giving Dawn the low down. Claribel nodded a few times, reaching into her own apron to snag a cookie or two, and even offered Dawn one a few times. Martha was the ringleader of the group, and Dawn began to see that they were the sort of welcoming committee.

"Did you hear that Cash has finally asked out Mabel? Bless her heart, don't know a thing about dressing up all fancy like. I told her, I did, 'Mabel,' I said, 'you just go on in there and show them how we roll around here.' She thanked me kindly, she did. Nice woman, Mabel, have you met her?" The question startled her out of looking for whoever Mabel was when Martha patted her on the hand.

"Honey, don't even try to get us all straight. We're a large and motley crew, we are."

"Like the band?" Again, Dawn never got to answer Mary, but Claribel started humming a song by the band in question. If this wasn't happening to her, Dawn would swear that someone was making this all up. "Oh. I almost forgot to tell you. What was it? Mary? What did I need to tell her?"

"I don't know, dear, but when it comes to you, I'm sure you'll remember." The needles never stopped clacking, and Dawn just watched them fly through the ball that was getting smaller by the row. "I'd like to come work for you."

Dawn looked around and then at Mary when she paused in her work. "Me? I don't have...well, Sloan and Jack seem to think I have a business, but I don't know yet."

"You'll have it if they have anything to do with it. They're very nice, but very pushy." Claribel started playing an air guitar, and Dawn smiled. Her humming had turned into words now, and she was nearly head banging with it. Mary smiled when Claribel got up to dance. "She does have a way with a guitar, don't you think? Don't tell her, but me and Martha are getting her one for her birthday. Lessons, too, if we can swing it."

"That would be nice." Mary smiled at her like she'd just given her permission or something. "Is it always like this?"

Dawn meant the way everyone seemed to pitch in and help, but Martha shook her head before answering. "No, dear, we're usually much nuttier. You caught us on a good day."

The laugh started low in her belly and made its way up to her mouth. It spilled out and seemed to make her entire body just simply feel good. She didn't think they were joking with her, or even putting on a show. These women were just nuts.

~~~

Ellis kept an eye on Dawn all night. And when the ladies three sat down next to her, he nearly went to get her. But Hunter stopped him. His brother laughed when Dawn looked around for him.

"She'll do just fine. And I've no doubt that you're going to hear her opinion about you not telling her about the pack." Ellis asked him who would tell her. "They will. I'm telling you that if there is something that you want everyone else to know, those three are going to be the ones that will spread it. I never seen a group of women with more solid information than those three."

"Gossips." Hunter told him that they weren't gossiping if it was the truth. "And who told them about this pack that I may or may not be taking?"

"Who knows? They might not even be sure themselves, but all they need is someone to confirm or deny it before they'll do their work. And I'm betting that one or more of them will have her convinced that she should do this jelly thing, too." Ellis watched the four of them for a few more minutes as Hunter continued. "She's going to do it, isn't she?"

"I don't know. She wants to. When we were talking about it today, she seemed to fluctuate between saying yes and telling Sloan to kiss her ass. Her words, not mine." Ellis grinned. "I think she'd do it, too, if she didn't want to. I'm telling you, every day she surprises me a little more. She's one hell of a woman."

"They all are. And if Dawn does this, which I'm betting she does, I want a family discount. Damn, Ellis, have you had the blackberry jam? It nearly made me whimper." Ellis told him to wait until he had some of her pickles. "Pickles? Christ man, you'll never have to work again if she does this. You realize that, don't you?"

"I don't care if I have to work for the rest of my life, so long as she's happy." Hunter told him he felt the same way with Sloan. Changing the subject when Dawn started to laugh, he looked at Hunter. "What have you heard about Combs and his wife? Shawn seems to think the man is about half baked. And that part is underdone."

"Good way to put it. And his wife, while a real bitch, is just as stupid. And I don't mean that in a derogatory way. I honestly think they're stupid." Ellis and Hunter moved deeper into the woods for privacy. "What do you know about her father? Anything come up on that yet?"

"No. Nothing. And Shawn told me about the policy that her mom had taken out on her in the event that she died before Dawn did. Apparently, they all think she knew that she was sick but never said a word. By the time they figured it out, she was too eaten up with cancer to have been saved. But she did fill out the paperwork to have her belongings sent to Dawn when she passed. Shawn is supposed to go up there Monday to claim them for her." Ellis told Hunter how Dawn felt about it.

"I don't blame her for not wanting to see it. But it might give her the information she needs to find her father." Ellis asked his brother why that was important. "It's not really. Not in the long run, but I think she might want to know someday. And your children might benefit from knowing, too. You just never know."

"No, you don't. But I'm not going to push this on her. She's stressed enough as it is."

Ellis made Hunter promise that if Dawn didn't want to look into it any more, that they'd drop it. Hunter said he could live with that. Ellis asked him what he'd been wanting to ask all night but just didn't know how.

"Do you...please don't bullshit me, Hunter. I really want to know, okay?" Hunter nodded. "Can I do this? Run a pack on my own? I know that I'd have Dawn at my side, but do you honestly think I can do this?"

Hunter watched the group of kids running around with the glow sticks that had been brought out just after dark. He smiled when one of them made a little girl scream by telling her it was a snake, and then the darling little girl punched him right in the nose. When they both stopped laughing, Hunter turned to him.

"When we first moved here, you guys tricked me into being alpha. I had neither the desire nor the gumption to be anything but one of the owners of Emerson Construction. Do you know who I thought would be the alpha?" Ellis told him Dad. It would have been a perfect fit. "No. You. You're more alpha than me. Hell, you're going to make two or more of Mike. He has neither the heart for it nor the muscle to put behind it. It's why the pack is in such trouble. And why a lot of them are leaving it for better grounds and more control from their pack leader."

Embarrassed that his older brother would say such a thing, especially about him, Ellis looked away as he spoke. "Mike said that nearly twenty percent have asked to leave. That's a huge number for such a small pack." Hunter nodded. "Are they coming here? Pledging to you?"

"Some have asked. But I told them that I'd have to think about it. We're about as big as I want to be. I'm giving you time to decide if you want it. Mike told me today that he's done. That his son wants him home and his wife is begging him to give it up." Hunter looked beyond him and stared at something only he seemed to be able to see. "I talked to Addie about it as well. She said that you'd have to hurt Mike for it."

"I can't do that." Hunter nodded. "I like the man. Respect him, too. If I have to fight him for the right to be pack alpha, it's not worth it."

"All right. But if you don't hurt him for it, draw first blood—and she seems to think it's only a small amount—then next month he'll be dead." Ellis shook his head, and Hunter nodded. "Someone else comes along that fights him and wins. Everything is broken up then. The pack is...everyone in it is destroyed."

Ellis looked at Dawn, who was dancing with Claribel and having a good time. He knew that Claribel had lost her son recently to a horrific accident, and she'd been barely functioning until Mary and Martha had taken her in and got her straightened up. It was the way they did things in his pack, the way he wanted to do things in his own. Take care of each other no matter what happened.

"I've asked...well, you know who I asked. Addie said that this other alpha, the one that takes the pack if you don't, he'll kill them all in a rage so huge that bodies will be torn apart so badly that it will be difficult to tell who is who. Women, children, anyone that is left will be dead." Ellis asked Hunter if he took this, would he fight the man as well? "I don't know. She can only see one future at a time, she told me. And it's not always complete. But this she seemed to be certain of."

"I'll talk to Dawn tonight, and then Mike. I'll give you an answer before we leave." Hunter told him that would be good. "Hunter? Will you do me one favor while I'm thinking about this? Will you please make sure, if anything happens to me, that Dawn is safe? I mean, if this other wolf comes for me, will you please make sure that Dawn isn't killed, too? You know what a new alpha will do to the female alpha."

"I do and I will. But you have to promise me the same. If I should be challenged and lose, you make sure that Sloan and my child are taken care of as well." They shook on it, and Ellis went to find his mate. He needed to touch her right now, and then he wanted to take her into the woods and fuck her until she couldn't move. Him either for that matter.

His plans changed when he walked up to her and she wrapped her arms around him. Ellis realized that he'd never danced with her, and when the music started playing a slow song, he swayed back and forth with her in his arms.

"So, we're going to be pack alphas, are we?" He nodded against her head and told her that he was going to talk to her tonight. "Martha said that you and I will make great leaders. And Mary wants to come and work for me when I open my production line. Claribel wants to answer the phone."

"Claribel has had some upset in her life, and it might be good for her to be your secretary." Dawn told him that was good because she'd hired all three of them. Ellis laughed. "Good. Anything else they told you that I might have to explain myself for?"

"Yes. Well, maybe not you, but someone will. Your sister-in-law sent a crew up to our place and started our new home. Did you know that?" He told her he didn't and started looking for Sloan. "I suppose I should have figured she'd do something like that. Addie, I mean. She said that she'd put the land in my name when I first moved there all those years ago. That I had done her a favor by staying alive for you."

"I'm glad she did that for you as well, but Addie is building our home for us?" She nodded against his chest. He lifted her chin up and looked at her. "How does she know what we want?"

"Really? Addie knows everything." Which, Ellis supposed, she really did.

CHAPTER 10

Basil was standing outside the jail when Neva pulled up to get him. She'd been with him since she went and paid his bill, but had to go and get their car to pick him up. His leg was still bothering him, and he didn't want to make it bleed again. She kissed him on the cheek when he got in.

"We just have to find us a place to stay until our house is finished. I went by there yesterday and, boy oh boy, they sure have been doing it up right nice. The house not so much, but the yard is looking good. They went and pulled out all your daddy's old cars he was going to work on." Basil was going to work on them as well, and thought maybe he'd ask that Shawn person if he could have them back when they were all done out there. He asked if they could go by again.

There were large flatbed trucks in the road and two of them had big semis on the front of them, but nobody in them. When they were waved around them, Basil looked into his yard, thinking to see the house all spruced up and the yard moved. But it was gone.

"Where did they move our house to?" Neva tried to turn around to go back, but there just wasn't enough room.

When she did manage to get up the road enough to turn around, they had to wait in line while another big piece of equipment was unloaded. Basil was sure that he'd made a mistake and had just missed the house.

"You just probably missed it." He nodded at Neva, thinking she had to be right. Why would they move their house? It didn't make any sense. "Maybe they're putting it somewhere so we don't have to pay for a hotel while the yard is being fixed up."

Basil didn't think that was it either. The more he thought about it, the more he knew they had knocked it down if all that mess in the yard had been what he'd thought it was. Their house was completely gone, and he just didn't know what to think.

As they drove up to where their mailbox had been—it being laid over in the grass all smashed up—he stood looking at where the big pinching machine was picking up what he thought was his front door and putting it in a big dump truck. There was their stove too, all smashed up to hell and dumped in there. Basil looked at Neva, who was crying.

"They didn't tell me they was going to tear it down." She shook her head, and Basil patted her on the back. "I don't know what's going on, honey, I don't. They said that we had to go away and that they'd take care of the place. This ain't taking care of it, it's tearing it to pieces."

"Maybe they mean to build us a new one." He didn't think that was right either. These men looked like they were the kind that tore houses down, not put them together. "What are we going to do, Basil? I got all our things that we thought we wanted, but what can I cook on? And our old television didn't work that good, but it was all right. We don't even have the rest of our cans that we been saving."

One of the deconstruction guys was walking by him when Basil asked him to stop. "Can you tell me why they tore this house down? I mean, who said they could do that?"

"The order came from...let me look and I can tell you." When the man walked to his truck and stood looking at a clipboard, Basil told Neva they'd get to the bottom of this. "Mrs. Dawn Whitfield. And Ellis...no wait, that's been scratched out and someone changed it. Dawn Emerson and Ellis Emerson are the ones that's name is on the order. We were told to take it all down to the bare earth."

When the man walked away, Basil could only stand there and stare at what had been his home for all his life. His niece had done this. Dawn, the brat, had taken their house from them and left them with nothing but a bag or two of clothing. He tried to comfort Neva, but she was crying so hard that even with his sore leg, he nearly had to carry her to the car.

"She done this to us." He nodded at Neva when she started screaming at him about the darned girl. "What right did she have to come in here and tear up our house? And take your daddy's fine cars? We got nowhere to live now. They have to put us a new house in, Basil. It's the only one I know'd of all my life."

He didn't point out that a moment ago they were junk and now that they knew who had done this to them, they were fine cars. But he understood what she meant. The brat had done this to them.

"We have to make her give it back to us." Basil told Neva there was no giving them back anything; it was all gone. "She owes us, Bassie. What are we gonna do now that she done went and had our family home…? She killed it."

"And after us taking her in when we was just as happy to not have her here." He had never liked the girl and had told Neva that all the time. "Her momma was nothing but a whore, spreading her legs for whatever had a thing there to stick in her. Then, like I told everybody, she got herself in trouble with the law, and now she's dead. And what do we have? Nothing. Less than nothing. And all because we done bought her issue into our house when she was nothing more than a kid."

"And we didn't do nothing to her but give her a roof over her head. What did she do to thank us? This. This is what she done." Basil nodded, getting madder by the second. He hated to lose his temper. When he did…he didn't ever remember what happened when he did, but Neva had been hurt once, and he hardly ever let it go no more.

When his head started to hurt, like it did the night that the brat had run off, he put his hands over his eyes and let out long breaths. He had to think, and Neva wailing wasn't helping him. Rocking back and forth on the seat, he started to count like his own momma used to tell him to do. Just not hear nothing around him but the numbers floating through his head. When he got to fifty, about as far as he could count without messing up, he started again and began to feel better. But he looked over at Neva and knew that he'd blacked out again.

"You hurt me, Bassie. Why?" Her nose was bleeding badly, and her mouth was all beat up, too. He wanted to tell her that he'd not done it, but he knew better. And he hated himself for it.

"I don't know, love. I don't know. It's all her fault." He handed her a few of the napkins that were in the glove box. "Here you go, just keep it from bleeding too much. I'm so sorry. You know how I get when I'm upset."

"I know." She was sobbing now, and his heart broke. "We have to make her put things to right, Bassie. It's the least she can do for us losing everything we had. We don't even have a couch to sit on no more. And your favorite chair is all gone, too. All them things that we saved and saved for. We don't even have a table to eat on. What will we do?"

Basil tried to think, but the pounding in his head started to make his belly hurt. Getting out of the car, he tried pounding the pain out of his head on the hood, but all that did was made him dizzy. He had to do something or he might hurt someone again. When he started walking, just going back toward town, his leg hurt, but he thought it was better than hurting his Neva. She was his wife, and he didn't want her hurt no more.

He had no idea how long he walked. His leg had started hurting almost right away, so he'd concentrated on that and not his head. When he came up on the gates that had locked him out of the place where he knew that the brat was, he walked around it and into the yard. Someone had been cleaning up here, too, but the house was still there.

The yard was mowed and there were new rocks on the drive. He walked around the yard to the back, and could see that someone had been working in what he thought was a garden. Going to the big barn, he tried to pry open the doors, but the lock was getting in his way. He was still walking around it to see if he could get into it when Neva came up to him.

"You still think she is around here?" He nodded, certain about it now. "Then I think we should take her house, too. I can't drive one of them big things, can you?"

"No. I don't even know how to drive at all. You know that." She nodded and stared at the house. "We could live here, I guess, but I'm betting that she's around here someplace."

Neva went to the house door and slammed her considerable weight against it. The door splintered under her weight, and when she stood up, he rushed to her side to see that she was all right. Other than her hip being a little sore, she told him she was fine as rain.

"Yeah. Let's have us a look around. We might just find us a way to get to that niece of yours." Basil was sad that she'd put it all on him, but she was right, it was his niece. So as they entered the house, the first thing they saw was a big bowl of apples on the counter. "We should see if there's something for us to take first. They sure did take all our stuff."

It took them over an hour to find all the stuff they were going to take from the house. Food had been important for them since they'd have to be living out of their car, he supposed. And he was pretty sure that there was no way they could just live here. There were too many people here now. As he got stuff from the refrigerator, Neva came rushing to the kitchen with an envelope.

"It is her. Damned if I wasn't right. This is her house, and she's been right here all this time. Right here under our noses." Basil took the envelope that had Dawn Whitfield on the front of it. It was a bill for the electric, and he could see by it that she'd been paying her bills every month.

"She wasn't helping us with all her money. Why not? We sure could have used some of this that she was paying off this bill for. Where was our cut?" Neva said that she didn't know, and Basil got angry again. "This just ain't right. Not right at all. First, her momma just drops her into our lap without as much as a nickel to her name. Then, she goes and runs off like we done her wrong or something. What are we supposed to do now?"

It wasn't true that she'd been dropped in their lives. In fact, Basil and Neva had decided not to take her in until they told them that they'd be paid by the government to do it. And they'd get all kinds of health discounts, too, should they need them. And the food stamp card. That was the real deal there. Free food.

"We should burn it down." Neva looked so happy at that thought that Basil was nodding before he could think of a single reason they shouldn't be doing this. "Yeah, burn it down with all her pretties in it. Just like she had them do to us."

Basil began dragging out the blankets that they'd filled with the stuff they were going to take. The more he thought about it, the better it sounded. When the last of it was out of the house they had themselves a meal of a big slab of ham and some bread that had been in the icebox. After a bit, they decided that it was time to take care of her house and the pretty things that they'd leave inside. Neva had taken the empty jars in the window, and he'd found himself a few things, too, that would start them on a collection again.

Neva started upstairs 'cause she could get around better, and he started putting a match to everything he could find. By the time Neva came down the stairs, he had a nice roaring fire going to most of the house.

~~~

Ellis hung up the phone and leaned against the wall. Christ, how the hell was he going to tell Dawn? He turned when he heard someone come into the room and looked at Sloan. She was smiling and rubbing her belly, but frowned before he could say anything to her.

"What's happened? Where's Dawn? Do I need to call people in?" His dad walked in the door just as he was ready to tell her what had happened, and he hugged him. The guy who had called him, one of the workers at the site, had said that he'd talked to an older gentlemen first.

"It's all gone." Ellis nodded, feeling tears fill his eyes. "Oh son, I'm so sorry. I'm so very sorry. Why would anyone do that to her? Such a nice little thing, too."

"Someone had better tell me or I'm going to get pissed. And you know how I am when I get pissed." Ellis couldn't talk, couldn't make his throat loosen up to say the words, but his dad could and turned to her.

"Their house was set fire to late yesterday evening. It's gone, all of it. Manning said that there wasn't even a speck of nothing left that they could have saved." Sloan sat down and started crying as well. "The couple that did it had tried to rob them first, he thought. Taking most of the food and other things out before they did the deed. But the fire was so hot, so fast that they barely made it away before that, too, was consumed. Manning called the police, but they were long gone by the time that anyone got there."

"She...she's going to be devastated when I tell her." Ellis looked at his dad when he sat down with them. "Our house isn't even started yet, just the foundation. What the hell are we going to do? And there's nothing but her things she brought here with her. She'll have to go shopping again. She hates that."

He was babbling, and everyone seemed to know it. Getting up to go to the stairs to tell her, he stopped when he saw her standing there in her robe. One look at her and he just started crying again. Sobbing out what had happened, he held her while she cried as well. He wasn't much for tears, but this had gotten to his heart in a way that made him think of how fragile things were.

"Everything? All my...everything?" He nodded, in better control of himself now that he'd had a few minutes. But she was still dealing with the pain, and he held her on his lap while sitting right there on the stairs. "Who would do such a thing to me? I've never.... My aunt and uncle did this, didn't they?" She looked at him.

"They were spotted leaving the house just as the smoke came out of the roof. Manning, a man on site that's working on our home and a friend of my dad's, said that they were dancing in the yard with some of the food from the house in a blanket. When a piece of the house fell onto it, they ran like all hell was after them. The police have someone out looking for them."

Dawn didn't move or speak for several minutes. Ellis just held her, telling her how sorry he was that this happened.

"I didn't have much. Not hardly anything at all, but it was stuff that I'd made or had fixed up to make work for me. Clothing, I guess. And some of your stuff. I guess it's a good thing we hadn't taken anything there yet, huh?" He told her that they'd start fresh. "Yes. Fresh is good."

She got up and moved to the kitchen. Dawn started moving around the kitchen looking like she was getting ready to fix them something to eat. Ellis didn't have the heart to tell her that he really wasn't that hungry. He didn't try to stop her when she pulled out a skillet, and when Sloan and Hunter's cook came in, he stayed out of her way as well. By the time she was mixing up a batch of what he knew were biscuits, the rest of his family was there.

They all pitched in making breakfast. His dad set the table, and Sloan helped him. Hunter was in and out of the room, making calls, handling things that needed to be taken care of. By the time they sat down, a huge breakfast laid out for them, Dawn was smiling again. Sadly, but smiling all the same. And the food was filling and comforting, too.

"They're going to work on the house as much as they can. Graham has consented to send the crew working on his house up as well. And Dan has a crew going up in an hour." Dawn nodded at Hunter as he continued. "We know who did this, and Mike has put out a warrant for their arrest. He thinks by nightfall they'll have them both."

"They did this because of the work being done where they lived. One of the men on site there said that he'd talked to an older couple a couple of hours before they heard the sirens. He said that the man was shocked to see the house gone, and then he'd asked who had done it." Addie said she was sorry before she continued. "The land is in both your names, and when he asked him, the guy didn't know not to tell them it was owned by Dawn Whitfield and Ellis here. I had crossed out your name on the bottom of the work order, but it was still at the top of it. He said that he corrected it, but he was sure now that they knew who you were by that name."

"So they find out that their niece, who had been abused by them for most of her childhood, owned the land that was signed over to her, and decided to burn my house down, too." No one said anything, and Ellis wasn't sure if Dawn was just speaking or really wanted answers. "Where will we live until we have a place to stay?"

"Here. With us." His dad looked over at Hunter, who nodded along with Sloan. "You can stay here, and when the garden is ready here, you can help show some of them fancy ideas to me and Sloan, so we can have as good a garden as you do."

"But for now, we're going to have to start getting things going for tonight." Everyone looked at Sloan when she stood up. "We're going to put our best face on, step out in style, and make some money for the abused children in this area. And after today, I think we should about double our efforts to make this the best damned charity event in the entire country."

As the women scattered to do their things, Ellis sat at the table trying to think why the hell someone would burn another person's house down. He looked up when his dad hit him in the back of the head.

"What the hell did I do?" His dad sat down and glared at him. "Dad? I didn't burn down the house. I didn't do anything to warrant you hitting me."

"Propose to her." Ellis sat up straighter in his chair, and Hunter laughed as his dad continued. "Do I have to do everything for you boys? Gosh darn all mighty. What do…are you going to marry her?"

"Yes. I already asked her, and she—" His head bounced forward again. "What the hell are you doing?"

"I didn't see no ring on her finger." He turned to Graham and Lee, who had just gotten into town last night. "Did either of you see a ring on her finger? Hunter, did you see one?"

"No, Dad, I didn't see one. I wonder why that is, since he asked her and all." Ellis made a mental note to tell Sloan something really horrible about her husband. And if he didn't know anything bad, he was going to make it up to get back at him.

"Why don't you go into town and I'll help you pick out a ring?" Ellis glanced over his dad's shoulder, and both Luke and Hunter were shaking their heads at him. Dad turned in time to see them both doing it, and he glared at them. "I had to help these idiots, too, and see the thanks I get? No respect for the elderly. I tell you, it's a sad, sad world."

"I have a ring." Everyone turned to look at him, and Ellis flushed. "I mean, I have it ordered. I did it before we left to come here. I'm supposed to pick it up in two hours."

His dad stood up and tapped his foot. Ellis wasn't sure what he wanted so he stood up too. At least he figured if he was standing, his dad couldn't hit him as hard. Ellis looked at the rest of his brothers before his dad started speaking in a tone that made him think he was talking to idiots, the lot of them.

"Get your coats on, boys. Make sure you've peed before we get into the car." Ellis started to laugh at them, scrambling to do as he'd said. "Don't laugh, boy, you're buying lunch for us all."

The trip in was made with Ellis driving Luke's car, and Luke and their dad in the back seat. Graham was up front with him and Lee; Hunter and Jarrett were in the other car.

They'd had to tell their mates that they were going into town. Ellis told Dawn that he'd be back soon, that he had to get his tux.

"Don't start off lying to her." He looked at his dad when he spoke. "Once it starts, there's no stopping the lengths that you have to go to unravel them."

"I am getting my tux." His dad smiled. "Dad, I love you very much for thinking so much of Dawn. You do know that she loves you, right?"

"I do. And I love all my girls, too." He looked over at Luke. "Even if some of you haven't made me a grandda yet. I'm hoping your brother gets on the band wagon a bit faster than you did."

"As a matter of fact, we're adopting a little boy next month." Ellis and the rest of them congratulated Luke, and he smiled. "We were going to tell you all tonight at the ball, but I think we could all use a pick-me-up. Jack is telling the others, too. His name is Kelly and he's six. He's half-wolf, but his mother just doesn't...she's giving him up, and he has to go through the screening process before we can take him. She's giving up all rights to him."

"Kelly, huh? And he's six?" Luke nodded at his dad. Luke turned in his seat to talk to Dad easier. "About the right age for me to take fishing, don't you think? And he'll be all ready for it by summer, too. I'll have to get him a pole and stuff. You think he'll take to the water okay? I can get us a boat, just the two of us."

His dad talked about all the things he and Kelly were going to do all the rest of the way into town. Luke turned and looked at Ellis as they pulled into the parking lot of the mall. When they were getting out, he hit him in the shoulder.

"You'd better get busy, little brother. I'm ahead of the game now."

Ellis sat there for several seconds after Luke got out of the car. And when Ellis got out, he had a plan. Not only was he going to make up a story about Luke to tell Jack, but he was thinking that he needed to add a prison term in there somewhere. The ideas and possibilities were endless. Yes, sir, he thought, his brothers were in deep shit as far as he was concerned.

CHAPTER 11

Basil wiped a wet cloth over Neva's head again. She was soaking wet and she was freezing. He had no idea what to do, but he was sure she was dying. When she said his name in the faint voice again, he moved closer to her and kissed her forehead.

"I don't want to die, not here." He sobbed a little. "I think you should just take me to the hospital now. I think they can fix me."

"I'll call them right now." He didn't, but she nodded at him. This was the third time she'd asked to be taken to the hospital, and he'd lied to her each time. They were wanted, and if he took her to the hospital, he was pretty sure that the cell he'd had before would be much nicer than the one they'd get now.

It was her heart, he knew that. They'd been running for their very lives when she'd told him that she wasn't feeling well and just dropped over. He'd stayed with her until the police and fire trucks had come. Then he'd run into the woods and hid. It was not the right thing to do, and Basil felt horrible about it. But when he'd gone back to get her, sure she was dead, she'd been feeling well enough to get up and walk. That's when he knew that things were not right with her.

Her walking had been off. When he'd tried to get her to walk in a straight line, she'd go to the right a little until she was walking in the wrong direction. And her mouth looked all funny. Sort of like his momma's did when she'd come home from the hospital. Saggy like.

And now her breathing was all harsh, like she had a terrible cold in her chest. Basil sobbed when she asked him again if he was going to call her an ambulance.

"I will."

When she closed her eyes, he knew it wasn't going to be long now, so he left her there. It wasn't *if* she was going to die now, it was *when*. And the way she was breathing told him that if he was going to get her help, even to have somebody bury her body, he'd better do it now. He moved to where a man was standing at the side of the road with a phone to his ear and waited for him to close his phone before he spoke.

"My wife is dying." The man looked around, then back at him. "In there. We got to here before she said that she ain't gonna be able to move no more. Do you think you could call her an ambulance for me? I'd sure appreciate it."

"Your wife is in that building and she's dying? Is it a drug overdose? " Basil broke down then, dropping to his knees even as the man called for him. "They want to know your name and hers."

"Her name is Neva, Neva Combs. I'm her husband, Basil." The man repeated the information in the phone, and Basil heard him say that he wasn't going to wait around. When he closed his phone again, he looked at him.

"They're on their way. And they said for you to wait here. The police will have some questions for you." Basil nodded, and as soon as the man was across the street, Basil starting walking away from his love and her body.

Basil watched from down the street. Just as he'd walked into the alley, the ambulance had gone screaming by him. He knew that they were going to find her dead, and when they came out a bit later with her body all wrapped up in a big black bag, he sat down and cried his heart out. Or at least what was left of it. The rest was in that bag with his Neva.

There was nothing left for him, he thought some time later. His body hurt from sitting in the same position for so long, and when the ambulance left the building that they'd been in, he watched as the police started making their way to his side of the street. It was only a matter of time before they caught him. He knew this as surely as he'd been sitting there thinking.

Walking again, he thought of all the things that had gone wrong at the house, the brat's house. The house had been old, so the fire had caught really quick. And the men that had been working on that land had come up on them so fast when they'd been enjoying the house going up that he'd nearly wet his pants, he'd been so scared. Neva had hit one of them with her shoe, and they'd laughed a little about that, too, just before she fell. Basil felt another sob coming on and bit his lip to keep from letting it go. Looking for a place to stay off the streets and warm, he walked into the first place that was open. It just happened to be a bar.

He watched the news in the bar that he'd entered; his picture and that of his Neva were all over the news. Either the people in the bar didn't care who he was or they didn't see him, but Basil was able to order himself a beer, the cheapest thing the man said there was to drink. Not that he'd touch it; the stuff made his head pound too much when he only took a sip or two of it.

When the bartender told him it was closing time, Basil wondered where the time had gone. No one was hurt around him and the bartender didn't seem to be afraid of him, so Basil figured that he'd only been napping and not letting his temper get ahold of him. He moved out into the street, only just realizing that he had nowhere to sleep tonight.

He made his way back to the building where he and Neva had been, but the yellow tape all over the place and the lone cruiser made him think twice about that. He had no idea how far he was from his home. But when he thought of that, he realized that it was gone, too.

"Everything I love is gone." Moving to the building across the street, he tried not to notice the couple having sex against the wall as he entered. He supposed that things like that happened in the city and was glad that he had a house.... Trying to fix his mind on something else, he wondered what he was going to do now.

This was all the brat's fault. Not all, he supposed. She didn't kill off Neva. Her heart had done that, as well as her running away from the men at the fire. If Dawn, of course, hadn't had their house all torn down, they would have been there and not burning down her house in the first place.

Basil leaned against the wall and was startled out of his thinking when a man handed him a blanket. It smelled really bad, but it was a good deal warmer than his little coat he'd had on when leaving the police station. Basil could not believe that just that morning he'd been in jail.

Thanking the man, he huddled down inside of the blanket, trying his best not to breathe through his nose. Turning his head away from the other groups of men and women getting settled in for the night, Basil cried himself to sleep. His Neva would never be there for him again.

~~~

Dawn was so afraid that she was going to fall on her ass. The shoes were actually comfortable, but they were much too high for her. And the more she tried to concentrate on not wobbling, the more she thought she did. Looking in the mirror again, she tried to think what Ellis would see when he saw her.

"You should see you the way we do." She looked at Sloan in the mirror as she sat at her dressing table. "You're very beautiful. Even Hunter says you're the type of beauty that wins contests, not marries his brother."

"I think he's as nuts as the rest of them are." Sloan laughed and said that she agreed with her. "Why do you suppose he's wanting to marry me? I know that's a stupid question to ask, but we're okay just living together now. Why do we need to have all that other stuff?"

"I said that, too. And Hunter said it was because we needed to make it legal in the eyes of humans." Dawn snorted. "My thoughts on that, too. But he did make a good point. He loves me and wants the world to know that I belong to him. He had to take a lot of hits with that, too. In the paper and online. They just couldn't understand why someone with my money would marry someone as...they called him mundane. Normal, and someone even said he was a gigolo."

"But you're happy, aren't you? I mean despite all the differences in your lifestyles, you're happy." Sloan turned to look at her, and Dawn flushed. "You must think I'm a real rube. I mean, I have nothing. Less than nothing, it feels like right now with everything gone, but he still loves me. I mean, it's not like I'm going to be contributing much to this relationship. And if he does take Mike's pack, I have no idea what to do there either. I can't even put together a nice dinner for more than four people without a full-out panic."

"Mary said that she, Martha, and Claribel are going to join your pack if Ellis does take it. And that they're going to work for you." Dawn nodded. "They're the oldest people in this pack, did you know that? And they know more about running one than anyone I bet could ever imagine."

"And that's another thing. I got that contract this afternoon. You do work fast." Sloan told her that when she saw something she believed in she didn't waste time. "Why do you believe in me so much? Is it because of Ellis? You're humoring me because I'm going to be living with your brother-in-law?"

"No. I wouldn't be in business very long if I let my feelings override my business sense. And let me ask you something. You say that you have no idea how this is going to work, right? The business you and I are going to do." Dawn nodded and sat on the bed across from her. "Why do you make the jelly year after year?"

"It's either that or the fruit goes to waste." Sloan shook her head. "Okay, then you tell me, Miss Know-it-all."

"You make it because you like doing it. It's okay to want to do that because it feels good. I like making money. I don't need any more. In several lifetimes, I could never spend all that I have. I enjoy it, and taking on a new business or two that may make some money too. It's an investment, yes, but it's also so rewarding to me when the company I've helped begins to show enough profit that they no longer need my support. That's the thrill of it for me." Dawn asked her how long she thought they'd be partners. "You'll be on your own before most companies I help are even halfway to getting things rolling. This event tonight will prove to you how much your jelly is going to succeed."

"I'm afraid." Sloan told her she'd better be, and Dawn laughed. "You are...I thought at first you were this scary alpha person. Not a bitch, though I'm pretty sure that you can be if you want, but this woman who knows it all and has a good head on her shoulders."

"But you don't think that now?" Dawn shook her head. "Now you see me as what? An over-round person that feels like the world is caving in on her at any given moment and that someone is going to see her for the fraud that she is?"

"You do feel that, don't you?" Sloan nodded and turned away from her. "No. I read up on you. Jack told me that I should. To get a better understanding of you and what you are. But you're none of those things you just said. No, what I see now is a woman who dearly loves her family, who wants the best for everyone even if that isn't what they think it is. And you are the most insecure person I've ever met. Including me. You want your child to be normal, but you have no idea what that is. And when you leave this house tonight to be on the spot, you'll do it because it's expected of you, not because you want to."

"That's about right. And you? What do you think I see with you?" Dawn shrugged, and Sloan laughed. "I see an equally insecure person, but someone who has more backbone than she thinks she does. And honey, you have a lot to have survived what you did living all alone for all these years. I, at least, had my wolves. You're brilliant, beautiful, and terrified more than you want anyone to know, and you're going to make a hell of an alpha bitch to Ellis's male."

Before she could tell her that she was right, on all of it, Jack and Addie came into the room. They were all getting dressed together and someone was coming to fix their hair and makeup. Dawn had no idea how to even begin on either of those projects, so she was glad to have someone helping her.

As soon as the hairdresser sat her in the chair, she tisked at her. "You needed a trim like ten years ago." She pulled her hair out of the ponytail holder and let it fall to her shoulders. "Pretty hair, but honey, you have to let it down once in a while. Oh my, what am I going to do with it?"

Jack winked at her in the mirror...she'd been told the same thing. But instead of a ponytail, Jack wore hers in a clip. Just as bad apparently. As the woman fussed with her hair, complaining about how it was stiff and unresponsive, Dawn let her do her thing. Ellis touched her mind just as the makeup artist came to do her face.

You should know that I might not be with you tonight because I'm going to kill my father. She laughed. *I swear to you, he has an opinion about everything and everyone. Did you know that the roast beef sandwich is not all that good for you? He's telling me this as he shoves a foot long one into his pie hole.*

You had a sandwich? I got to have a salad with chicken on it and a little dressing. We're supposed to not be bloated when we put on our dresses. Frankly, I'm going to need to eat something before the dinner thing tonight or I'm going to be lying on the floor from hunger. Just as unflattering, I think. He told her he loved her. *And I love you. Save me a few chips if you have any. I've not had any of those in years.*

I love pickle chips. That's what I'm having with my sandwich now. He moaned, and she wanted to hurt him. *There's going to be food there, did you know that? I mean a real meal of roasted chicken and rice something. Also there's a lot of finger food. Not usually my thing, but I'll make sure I load you a plate and carry them around for you to nibble on.*

Thank you very much. She closed her eyes when the woman fixing her makeup told her to. *I'm going to be all painted up. You might not know me when you see me. And my hair is a mess according to the stylist. I'm not allowed to put it into a ponytail anymore.*

I love it when we make love and your hair touches my naked skin. She shifted in her seat and told him to behave. *I want to see you in those heels I saw in the box. Just the heels and some of those stocking things that only go up to your thighs. Or better yet, do they make garters anymore? I'd love to see you in one of those and nothing else. When we leave this thing, I want to undress you. Peel your dress off you an inch at a time and kiss all the skin that I expose.*

Ellis, you are so not helping me. He told her that he wasn't trying to. *All right then. When we get back to the house tonight, I'm going to show you the pantie and bra set that I'll have on tonight. Creamy lace that barely holds anything in. And my nipples get so hard in it when it rubs against them. It's hard to concentrate on anything, they're so hard.*

You are so going to pay for that. She giggled. *I might have to find us a really dark corner and ravish you before the bidding begins. Or perhaps while the bidding is going on. That way the auctioneer will cover your screams when I make you cry out.*

She was aching. And wet. Closing her legs together, she tried to think of anything but what he'd said to her. When he touched her mind again, she knew that she was going to tackle him as soon as he came near her. But there was something different this time. He felt tense and sorry about it. She nearly asked him what was happening when he spoke.

Honey, they just found your aunt's body.

Her entire mind froze up. He continued talking, but she couldn't hear him anymore. Nothing was getting through to her, and it wasn't until she was slapped that she felt like she could breathe again.

"That's it. Take in as much air as you can." Sloan was cursing as she held her shoulders. "Breathe, Dawn. Don't pass out on me."

"I'm okay now." Sloan watched her. "I am. I...my aunt is dead. Ellis just told me, and I sort of lost it there for a minute."

"You scared the fucking shit out of me." Dawn told her she was sorry. "I'm sorry about your aunt. I truly am. But don't ever do that again. I thought for sure you were having a heart attack. And contact Ellis...I think you scared him more than me."

Ellis? He told her he loved her. And that he was sorry. *I'm sorry I scared you. I just...I don't know what happened, but it was like I zoned out for a minute.*

Sloan said that you stopped breathing. Not dying, but just were not breathing. I'm so sorry, baby. I should have told you better. It was just on the news here and I thought you should know before someone called you. Dawn told him she was all right now and to tell her what was going on. *They're saying heart attack. They were called by someone who said that her body was in an abandoned building and that she was dying. Your uncle apparently waved down this guy and asked them to call for him. He gave his name and hers to him and he called it in. Neither of them hung around until the police got there. I'm so sorry.*

I wonder what will happen to Uncle Basil. I mean, he wasn't able to drive or anything. She was babbling and stopped. *The police are looking for him, no doubt.*

Yes, but not for this. The fire. She'd tried to forget about that and told him so. *Yeah, I don't blame you there. But our house is coming along and we'll be able to move in sooner than we thought now. Hunter and Sloan are helping out with that too. I know that we'll owe them for the rest of our lives, but it's great that they're doing this.*

Ellis, I want a baby. He didn't say anything, and she felt silly. *I know that I'm sort of throwing this at you, but I want your child. I want a family of our own. We don't have to have a lot of kids, just one or two, but I do want your baby. Please?*

I was going to talk to you about that. I was. It's just been so...I want to see you big with our baby. I want to see you nurse him or her, have them with us. Dad was saying tonight that he wants a bunch of grandkids. Did you know that Luke and Jack are adopting? I think that's wonderful for them. His name is Kelly and he's six. We're all thrilled for them.

By the time she was ready to go, she was a mess. Not her appearance in the mirror, but the way she felt. Her aunt had been in her life when she'd been younger, of course. They had both treated her like crap, but she was about all the family she had in the world and now she was gone. And the fact that her uncle was out there, without his Neva, made her wonder how he was faring as well. The man had loved his wife more than anyone ever had, she thought.

Dawn had on her cape when she came down the stairs, and was nearly at the bottom when she saw Ellis. If ever a man looked better in a tux than him, she thought she'd die from looking. Then the rest of his brothers joined him. And when Cash stood in front of his sons, it was as if the heavens had opened up and showed what real handsomeness was.

When Sloan and the others stopped beside her, Cash laughed. "Damn, but ain't that about the prettiest bunch of women you ever done did see? And they're all mine tonight." One of the brothers cleared their throat, and he turned to them. "You tell me that I can't go into the shindig with them hanging on my arms, and I'll buy everything I can there tonight and make sure you guys split the bill."

"All right, but the first dance is with our wives, if you don't mind." Cash seemed to consider Hunter's words before he said okay. "Dad, you are right, however. They are the most beautiful women in the world, and they do belong to all of us."

After they went by and picked up Mabel, who looked as nervous as she said she felt, they got on their way. The limo ride was short but very nice. Dawn was nervous, but not so much now that she had Ellis with her. Cash made comments all the way over, and when he saw her shoes, he had to joke about them as well.

"I'm thinking that should I need to drill a hole in a wall or two, those would start the screw for me." She giggled when he held her foot up for everyone to see. "I don't know how you women walk around in those things. I know that they make you look all sexy and stuff, but that's gotta hurt some."

"You have no idea. I've been practicing in them since I got them. And I did fall when I tried them on. Jack made fun of me." Jack laughed and said that she took pictures, too. "See, Cash, I think that you're the only one who loves me right."

"You stick with me and Mabel, darlin', and you and I will be just fine and dandy."

When the limo stopped, the men got out first. Dawn, from her position near the opposite door, could see that there were pictures being taken and the noise level was amazing.

As soon as Ellis put his hand into the car to help her out, she had a slight panic attack, but he stuck his head in and winked at her. "You gotta come out sooner or later. And there's food in here. I called ahead and have a plate waiting for you at the door."

"You promise?" He nodded and put out his hand again. "I love you. And if I really mess up and get your picture plastered all over the papers about how you are in love with an idiot, you'll know that much."

"You're the best thing that has ever happened to me, and if anyone asks, that's what I'm going to tell them, too." When she was out and standing next to him while thousands of camera flashes made her blink, she felt pretty. Not just pretty, but loved as well. As they entered the big building, Dawn knew then how the rich and fabulous made things work.

CHAPTER 12

The glitter and the glitz had never seemed so bright to him. Ellis was seeing it all though Dawn's eyes and simply fell in love with all the beauty of it. As per arrangement, one of the waiters handed him a plate overflowing with little bits of food and sweets. And when he handed it to Dawn to sample, she started to cry.

"Honey, you mess up your makeup and Sloan will have my head. Christ, Dawn, you look amazing." She nodded and took a cheese and cracker from the plate, and he handed her a glass of champagne, too. "Not too fast until you eat more. I don't want you falling off your shoes either."

They walked around the room and, true to his word, he never left her side. His dad had walked in with him with Mabel on his arm, and then the two of them had moved to take on the crowd, as he'd called it. Ellis introduced Dawn to everyone, telling them that she was his future bride.

"This is amazing." He nodded and kissed her on the shoulder. "Who knew there were this many people to come out to this?"

"Addie said that people come from all over the world to her events. And they raise a great deal of money, too. She'll be working the crowd later, asking for people to remember what the event is for and who they're going to be helping. Did you want to see the donations she's gotten?"

They made their way into the room where tables and tables of things were laid out. There was a Jaguar in the middle of the floor and a Mercedes on the other end of the room, both of them fully loaded. "Most of the smaller items come with some sort of incentive. Like this one for a day spa. If you bid on this, you also get to have champagne for two, caviar, as well as dinner. Then there is this one, the one I want to bid on."

Ellis wanted the truck. It was a toy compared to what he used as his work truck. That one was made to be beaten up, driven through mud, and treated like another part of his job. This one had four doors, air conditioning, and leather, heated seats. The back end was coated in a heavy coating that would keep it from harming whatever was being hauled. The tailgate was heavy and made to be sat on, not just loaded on. But it was the art work that had him drooling over it.

He'd always been an Ohio State fan. He'd gone to college there, as had two of his brothers, even though they'd been living in another state. Ellis had been to every football game that he could manage, and had plans for a room in his house that would be devoted to nothing but football and his Buckeyes. He bled scarlet and gray. And this scarlet paint job with the gray trim said how much the person who had donated this baby loved them as well.

The mascot was featured on every door. Football leather hugged the steering wheel with laces, and the seats just begged to be caressed. The horseshoe stadium on the tailgate made him almost feel like he was right there. The art work was exquisite and extremely detailed. And the package didn't end there.

There was a grill in the back with four bagged chairs, as well as a giant cooler with the same logos on it and with the same colors. A scarlet table with gray legs on it could be folded up into a nice neat bag. And the topper was four season tickets to the entire new season that started in just a few months. Ellis thought the thing would go for a great deal of money.

"You like this?" He nodded, not turning to look at Sloan. Dawn had gone with Addie to look at her own donation. "You should get it."

"No. I can't. I want to, but it'll go for more than I can simply justify right now." She nodded. "Do you know who donated it? I'm assuming some person with too much money and a great love for football."

"Hunter did." He turned to look at her. "He did. He said that he'd like one for himself and said that if he wanted it, then someone else would as well. I'm getting him a truck like this for when our daughter is born. Please don't tell him."

"I won't. He's going to shit. You know that, right?" She grinned at him, and he laughed. "Ah, so that's the point. And what is he getting the mother of his child? Something equally wonderful, I'm betting."

"He is. I don't know what, but he said that I, too, was going to shit bricks. Do you think that it's a little over the top? Hunter had a blast with it. I think he's been planning this for a few months. At least since he met Addie. She brings out the best in him. You know what sort of loops she had to go through to have this drawn? They said in the future she can do art for them when they need it. Quite a feather in her cap, if you ask me."

Graham and Lee joined them. Lee had overseen the food at this thing as part of his donation, and he was fussing about an ice sculpture that had been put in the wrong drink. Apparently, that was a big deal. Ellis was laughing at him when his dad and Mabel came to stand next to him.

"Mabel, you look amazing. And now when I see you behind the counter at home, I'm going to know what a goddess you really are." Mabel smacked him on the arm and thanked him. "Dad, you really know how to choose your women."

"I do, I do at that. You got everything ready for your own woman there, boy?" He nodded and patted his pocket for what felt like the millionth time. "You know when you're going to make her happy? I'm getting really excited myself."

"I have it worked out." He did, and was slightly tense about that, too. "Just leave it to me. I've got it under control."

His dad just snorted and walked away. Ellis went to find Dawn, and she was talking to several women when he got to her side. She introduced him to the governor's wife and the wife of the senator.

"They were just telling me that they want my jellies when I go into production. I told them I had no idea when that would be, but they said that they'd wait." She smiled at him, but it was tight. "Your sister-in-law has already set me up a website and pictures. I think I might kill her."

The two women laughed, and the governor's wife patted Dawn on the arm. "I know Jack. When she gets something into her head, it's better to go with the flow than to try and rein her in. She's a little head strong. Just let me know when you're set up, darling. I want to be your first and best customer."

As they moved away, he looked at her basket of jellies. It really was a beautiful display, and he wondered who had done it. When Dawn spoke up, he thought for sure that Jack was going to be dead before the end of the night.

"She came right in here and told me to set this up. Like I had a clue what to do with it. There was a really nice woman who handed me a bag of this shredded stuff, and Mabel tied the ribbon on it. All I do at home is stick it in the cabinet. I do not go around decorating it for my table." He laughed and when she glared at him, he tried really hard not to laugh louder. "When did she become my boss, I ask you? Ordering me around...and the website? If these women hadn't shown me on their phone, I would have had no idea. It's pretty and all, but I don't have anywhere to do this."

"Yes you do." He took a step back when she turned on him. "Dad and I looked at a warehouse online for you today that was near our new house. I made an offer and they accepted. It was well below what they were asking, but it had been on the market for a while."

"You don't have that sort of money. Okay, you might, but I don't. I have to...I have to...." She looked at him. "I think I'm going to be sick."

Kicking off her heels, she took off running to the bathroom. He almost followed her, but Sloan stopped him.

He told her quickly what was going on, and she said she'd handle it.

"Just don't let Jack come in. I think there really will be bloodshed if she does." Sloan turned to look at him and smiled. "She's pushing her a little too fast."

"No, she's not. I'm keeping an eye on her. And she'll be just fine." She started away again but took Dawn's shoes from him when he picked them up. "Nice job on the building, by the way. Your dad said you got her one. So you know, I'm outfitting it for her. As a wedding gift."

There was no telling her no either, so he only nodded.

CHAPTER 13

Ellis watched the bidding wars. And that's exactly what it was. When something was put up that was in high demand, the wars began. Even people at the same table became a little insane when one of their table mates started outbidding them. He had a good laugh several times when a divorced couple were at it hot and heavy until they were outbid by another patron. Then the basket of Dawn's jelly came up. He watched her face as the men helping out tonight held it up for all to see.

The script was read like the man had had a bowl of it just before coming up in the stage. He told how it was homemade, the greatest thing since sliced bread. Then he told the audience that he already had a starting bid of five thousand dollars.

To be honest, Ellis thought it was either Addie or Sloan that had put in that bid. It would be something they'd do to boost her confidence, but the governor's wife stood up and said it was all hers. All hell broke loose after that, mainly between three woman; the senator's wife who he'd met before, the governor and his wife, as well as a woman that looked like she'd chew you up and spit you out into fiery pieces should you cross her. Ellis found himself rooting for her to win, fearful of would happen should she not.

As it turned out, the governor's wife had to settle for getting hers online. The dragon woman admitted defeat when the senator's wife declared herself the winner and walked away with the prize, handing two of the little jars to each of her opponents like a good winner.

Dawn turned to look at him, her face a study in stunned amazement. "That woman just paid eleven thousand dollars for six jars — six small jars — of jelly. Eleven thousand dollars."

"I saw that." She stared at the auctioneer, then looked back at him. "Honey, it's fine. It's for charity and you made a big hit with them. The governor's wife is going to order more from you, too. I'm not sure about the other woman, but I'd make her some even if you have to do it in our kitchen. I don't think we want her as an — "

"I don't think I can do this." She looked panicky, and he kissed her. Then he stood up. "Are you leaving me? Not yet please. She's going to realize what she's done and how much she's just paid for a little bit of fruit and sugar, and demand that I give her back her money. Not that I had anything to do with it, but she'll come after me all the same. I don't have that kind of money. Not even...my house burned down and all my cash was in there. I don't think it amounted to much more than a thousand dollars, but it's all I had. Please don't leave me, Ellis, I need you right here."

"That's what I'm counting on." Moving his chair out of the way, he turned hers to him. Then he went down on one knee. She looked around the table, and he could see that his family had gone quiet and were standing up as well. "Dawn Whitfield, will you be my wife? Will you marry me and make me happier than a man has a right to be? Will you sleep with me every night, wake with me in the morning, and hold me throughout the day? Will you keep me in your heart, as you've been in mine since the time I first saw you in my dreams all those months ago? I love you, Dawn. Will you please be my wife?"

He slipped the ring onto her finger and held her hand. She was crying and looking at him, but she'd yet to say yes. Ellis was terrified that she was thinking how to tell him no. When she leaned down and put her forehead to his, he knew she was turning him down.

"I have loved you since I first saw you searching for me in the woods. Even not knowing who you were or why you were looking for me, I knew that you were a man to love and to love well. I just never expected it to be me that you'd love." He closed his eyes, thinking of how much he loved this woman. "I will marry you, but you should know that I will love you with all that I have, for all my life. You will be forever first in my heart and on my mind. I will love your children, and care for you and them above all others. I love you, Ellis Emerson. Yes, I will be your wife."

"Now that's the way to propose to someone." His dad pulled him up from the floor and hugged him. "Ellis, I have never seen anyone do a proposal with such style and love. Your mother would be so proud of you. All of her boys."

His dad kissed Dawn and welcomed her to the family, and that's when Ellis realized that the entire room had been listening to them. Not only had the auctioneer stopped his fast talk, but everyone in the room had paused to see what was going on. And when Ellis pulled Dawn into his arms and kissed her, they all applauded and shouted out their congratulations. But Ellis held up his hand.

"I'm not finished." The room erupted in laughter. "What I meant to say was that I wanted this night to be special for my future wife. And in order for her not to have second thoughts about marrying me, I've taken this one more step."

Ellis nodded to the auctioneer, who turned to the band that had been playing quietly while they ate. When they started playing the wedding march, Ellis handed Dawn off to his dad and moved to the dais that the auctioneer had been using. Jack, the only other person who had known what he was planning, started directing people to where they needed to be. Soon it was apparent to the others in the room—they were at a wedding.

Sloan, Addie, and Jack were being escorted to the front of the room by his brothers; Lee and Graham, single for now, brought their own dates with them. It was, after all, a family affair. When his dad started toward him with Dawn, he stopped and asked for a second. Ellis wondered what he was doing when he whispered to Mabel. She dug into her purse and handed him something.

"Sorry, folks." He turned to Dawn as he continued speaking to the crowd in general. "I kinda knew that he was going to ask to marry my girl here tonight. Didn't know they'd be getting hitched, but I like his style. But I had Mabel there store something for me so I could give it to Dawn afterwards like. She sure is working out just fine in my little part of the world, just so you all know. But this here, this is fitting. A bride needs something old and something new. And this thing here fits both bills."

When he stepped back from her, Ellis saw what his dad had done. It had been his mother's locket. The chain long ago had been broken, and Ellis would bet that that was what his dad was referring to as the new. The locket was one that she'd worn all through his childhood. Inside it was a picture of Ellis and his mom taken the day he'd been born. Dad had given her one for each child she'd given him, their date of birth engraved on the front with the letter E.

"Oh, Dad."

Dawn sobbed to his dad and hugged him, and Ellis wanted to join them. But then she turned to him and told him that she loved him and wanted to get this done. Dad escorted her to him and started to leave them at the makeshift altar, but Ellis yanked him to him and hugged him tightly. In minutes, he and Dawn were united as man and wife, and his family had just gotten a good deal better so far as he was concerned.

As they made their way back to their table, everyone stood up and applauded again. Many of them hugged them both; some told him it was the best wedding they'd ever been to. The entire thing had gone off without a hitch.

As soon as they were seated, the auctioneer, not missing a beat, brought out the truck Ellis wanted and started the bidding at nine thousand dollars. He couldn't even look at it now, didn't want anything to come between him and his wife. When the auctioneer shouted "*Sold!*" and then told the price, Ellis nearly fell off his chair when Hunter told him congratulations.

"I love her. What did you expect me to do?" Hunter told him that was nice but not what he was talking about. "What?"

"The truck, it's yours." He looked at his family around the table as Hunter continued. "We all decided that if anyone was going to have it and it couldn't be me, then you should. So we decided on a price and that's what we did. It was Dawn's idea."

"You did this?" She shrugged when he asked her. "You had them buy me a truck? An amazing truck, but you had them buy this for me?"

"I knew you wanted it. It was all you'd been talking about since I met you. And since I have a new business partner, I asked for a little extra on my loan from her, and we decided that we'd all go in together. I had no idea I was getting married, so it's only fair that you didn't know my plans."

Ellis picked her up in his arms and swung her around the room. He'd never in all his life forget this night. When he said as much to Dawn, she told him he'd better not if he knew what was good for him. Laughing, he carried her out of the ballroom and down the hall to a room he'd scoped out earlier.

~~~

She was married. That was all that kept running through her mind when he rushed her out of the ballroom and down the hall. She wrapped her arms around his shoulders and smiled up at him.

"Are you planning to ravish me?" He nodded. "Not if I get to you first. I have plans myself, big boy. And none of it centers on wherever it is you're taking me."

He stopped. "What did you have in mind?" She asked to be set down. "Dawn, if I don't get to make love to you soon, I might have to hurt someone."

"Trust me, you will." She made her way to the doors and as she went, she kicked off her shoes and let her hair down out of the very beautiful coronet that it had been put in. Turning to look at Ellis as he stood there, she smiled at him. "I'm going to be naked by the time I get to the woods. And the moment I get into them, I'm going to be a wolf. A very needy, very wet wolf."

She was out the door and down the steps by the time she heard him curse. As she stripped out of her stockings and tossed them back in his direction, she was glad that this building was situated so close to where she wanted to be. Ellis was right behind her when she let her wolf take her.

She didn't run hard or even that fast. The thrill of the chase was what she wanted, and Ellis was giving her that. Even as he tackled her a couple of times, she knew that he was letting her get away. And when she finally stopped running, he was right there with her.

I love you. She rubbed her body over his, marking him with her scent. *I need you.*

I need you as well. He growled at her when she moved away from him. *You run now, and he might hurt you. My wolf needs to mark you after all my brothers touching you.*

As mine does you. She moved back to him, her body needy, but not desperate for his. *Ellis, please take me.*

He mounted her. It was fast, and he had her penned under him in seconds. Her wolf, even as needy as she was, still fought him, tried to bite him when he started fucking her. When Ellis's wolf sank his teeth into her shoulder, it was different than before. This one was a mark of possession and one that she welcomed. He came and she cried out when he tore at her flesh, then again when he bit her a second time on the opposite shoulder. His howl, dark and full of wildness, echoed around them, bouncing off the surrounding trees.

His demand that she shift had her leaving her wolf behind and letting her human self reach out for Ellis's body.

He didn't enter her like she needed. Instead, he buried his mouth over her pussy, sucking hard on her clit until she screamed out her release three times.

"Fuck me." He shook his head no as he knelt over her with his cock in his hand. "Ellis, I swear to Christ, I'm going to murder you if you don't take me."

"Suck my cock." Dawn stared at his cock, dripping with cum, as he continued to fist himself. "Take me into your mouth and let me come down your throat."

She moved to her knees as he leaned back and then sat on the ground. Dawn wanted to tease him, to lick him until he begged her to finish him, but her first taste of him had her wanting more. Needing more. Taking him deeply into her mouth, then swallowing him past the tight muscles in her throat, she felt his fingers curl into her hair as he fucked her this way.

When he tightened his fingers painfully in her hair, she knew that he was close. Cupping his balls in her hand, she held them, squeezed them gently until he cried out. His cum, hot and spicy, slid down her throat while he held her head to him as he emptied into her.

When he jerked her head up, pulling her into a kiss that took her breath away, he rolled them to her back, his body, his cock buried inside of her like a punch. She screamed when she came, but he never stopped as he suckled at her breast and took her to the edge twice more to have her dropped over all too soon. When he bowed back from her, his groin pounding his release inside of her, Dawn came again, marveling at the beauty of this man who was hers.

Ellis dropped onto her, his weight not heavy, but warm and comforting. When he rolled to his back, taking her with him, she felt his cock stir enough to let her know that he wasn't nearly finished with her. She lifted her head and looked down at him.

"I'm your wife." Ellis grinned but didn't open his eyes as he lay there. "I found out something that you might not know. As a shifter, my body works differently than yours."

"I should hope so. If it didn't, what we just did would have been a lot less fun for one of us." She smacked him on the bare chest. "Christ, I wish I could take you to a hotel and do this to you all over. Not much of a wedding night."

"This is absolutely perfect." She poked him gently when she saw a deer eating some of the new grass that was coming up. There was a nest of birds nearby that had him looking up with her. Several squirrels came out of their den as they lay there quietly. "We're among friends here. Creatures somewhat like us in that they're animals that like to be what they are as well."

As they watched the woods come alive, even this late in the night, he stroked her back with his fingers, giving her warmth with his own body. She felt his love even when he closed his eyes again.

"What did you mean when you said you're not like me?" He laughed. "I mean other than the obvious."

"I don't go into heat." His fingers stilled in their path down her back. "I can get pregnant whenever we want. I don't have to wait for the moon cycle like other shifters do."

"You mean you could be pregnant now?" She told him that she could be. "Like right now? You could be...we could be having a child, right now?"

"Well, not right now, but soon if you want." He nodded at her when she looked down at him again. "Do you want a child now, Ellis? We have no house, your job is in transition, and I don't have a pot to pee in. Do you want to have a child now?"

He rolled her to her back and looked at her. She wondered what he saw there, searching her face so intently. When he lowered his mouth to hers, kissing her gently and softly, he lifted his head and told her he loved her.

"To have a child with you would be the greatest dream I could have fulfilled." She nodded, and before she could tell him that was what she wanted, he continued. "I don't care if we have to raise our child in the barn on the property until the house is done. We could live with Sloan and Hunter until our baby goes to college. To see you round with our baby, get to see it suckle at your breast as you feed it, would make me the happiest man on earth. No, the happiest man in the universe."

"Then we should work on it now."

Ellis nodded and moved inside of her. His lovemaking was different this time. There was no sense of urgency; he took his time, bringing her to peak twice before he filled her again with his seed. This time when he held her, it was more like a cradle to her, his body wrapped around hers. Even as she dozed, napping lightly after coming so many times, she felt something she'd never in her life felt...security in the knowledge that when she woke he'd still be there and that he'd still love her.

Waking when the moon was over head, she yawned twice and woke Ellis. It was cold now that the moon was bright in the sky, and she hurried to find the bag that she'd left out here earlier today. They giggled like small children when they put their clothes on backwards, and laughed when they realized she'd forgotten to pack herself some shoes.

"I was in a hurry, all right? I didn't want anyone to know what I was doing." He offered to give her a piggy-back ride. "No. You take my clothing and I'll fly back to the house. We can't go back to the auction anyway."

He told her to be careful and that he loved her. Stripping down again, she was in the sky in a matter of seconds. Dawn loved to fly this way.

Dawn was waiting on the deck that was outside their room when Ellis opened the doors. She let her bird go and ran naked to the bed and jumped under the covers. Ellis joined her a few minutes later after securing the door and turning out all the lights. He held her much like he had in the woods, but she was warmer now to enjoy the love of it and not the necessity.

"Do you really want to have a baby right away?" Dawn told him that she did. "I do, too. As soon as we can. But if you don't mind, I'd also like to open our home to others. Maybe adopt, like Luke and Jack are."

"I'd very much like to do that." He nodded and held her tightly. "Ellis, how many children are we talking? You don't mean to adopt all those kids that they ran pictures of tonight, do you?"

The pictures of the children they were helping had been put up on a large screen television that ran all night. Jack had been against putting the photos of the children with their bruises and broken bodies, and Addie had agreed. The pictures were of the children that had been helped last year, all the goodness that had come from their donations.

Some showed them riding their first bike. There were several pictures of children at their first Christmas tree, their first restaurant, their first a lot of things. Most of the children, Addie had told her, were from broken homes, where there wasn't enough money and tempers were high. Plenty of children hadn't made it onto the role of pictures. A lot of them had died due to injuries from the people that were supposed to care for them, to give their lives for their wellbeing. A lot more had died from neglect.

"Five." She asked him five total or just five of the children. "Five of each. We should have five children of our own, and adopt five more to give them a family with us."

"You want ten children?" He nodded and smiled down at her. "All right, but the first one that pukes is all yours."

Three hours later they were woken from their beds to catch a flight to their home, and what she hoped would be the makings of a business opportunity of their own. Then they still had to deal with her relatives.

CHAPTER 14

Basil wandered around the yard that had once been his and Neva's. Now it was just a few piles of stone and a hole in the ground. He could still see where there had been cars parked for so long that the grass beneath them had long since died. The trees that had sheltered them had been shoved out of the way for the heavy equipment. And then there was the porch that he and Neva had sat on in the warmer months, looking at the wild animals that would come out to eat. Basil sat down on one of the larger pieces of equipment that had yet to be loaded onto the flatbeds that sat waiting for them.

He began talking to her, Neva. He knew that she was gone from him, but he still needed to talk to her about things. On the walk back to this place, he'd told her that he was going to die and be with her. Told her even how he was going to do it. But he didn't have the heart to do it once he got there.

"I really was going to lay under them big wheels. I know now that it would never have worked. They'd have seen me and then taken me off to jail. I don't think I'd do good in jail. There are too many bad people in there." Basil tried to shy away from the bad person he'd been by leaving his Neva, but it came to the front of his head then, and he thought about it again.

"I should have stayed with you. I know that now. I might have gone to jail, but then I wouldn't have left you all by your lonesome there when you needed me most. You were right there with me all the times I needed you, and I failed you when you needed me." He cried for a little bit, knowing what his momma would have said to him about grown men crying. But he missed his wife and knew that he was a bad person.

"I've been thinking on some things. I'm going to find that girl, Dawn. She might not like me finding her after all this time, but I'm not going to give it up. She don't owe me nothing like I been thinking all this time, but I want her to know that I think she should be helping me out with your funeral." He looked beyond what had been his yard to the woods beyond. "You think you'd like to be buried back there? Near that creek bed you and I used to go to when we was more able? I'd like that myself. Knowing that we got us some shade when we need it, and to hear them there crickets that we can hear in August."

He made his way to the creek now, knowing that it was gonna be all froze up still like it always was. Basil thought about the few times they'd been without power for one reason or another. Usually they'd not paid the bill, but they'd used the creek water to bathe in and to keep their stuff cold. Milk had tasted so much better coming out of the water when they'd done it that they'd decided to keep it cold like that all the time. But they hadn't. They'd both been too old and too lazy to make the trip back and forth to do it. But it was good when they had it.

He sat next to the water, surprised to see it flowing so well. There weren't any fishes in it yet—the water really was too cold, he supposed—but as he sat here, thinking about where he'd like to be buried, a couple of their deer came out of the woods for a drink.

When they were startled away by something only they heard, he talked to Neva again. "I got no way of bringing you out here, my love. Not one penny to my name. That check that that there lawyer said I could have is with you. You had it on you when you passed, and I never thought to get it. I suppose some guy in that ambulance is having himself a good time on it by now."

He heard the car come into the drive and realized it wasn't from his home, but that of his neighbors, the ones that he was sure were harboring Dawn. Not that he wanted her harmed no more, but he did need her help. Getting up, his body stiff and sore from all the walking he'd done, he made his way to where there was a building going up and men and women wandering around the property working. Basil stood there for several minutes, just watching the way they seemed to have some music playing in their heads and only they could hear it.

The woman and man that he saw coming out of the big barn made him hide behind a tree. He knew them; they were the couple that was living here the first time he'd been looking back here. And now they were the ones that were working on this place, too.

He watched them and thought of his own wife. He had no idea if they were married or not, but they were in love. The man couldn't stop touching her, and she kept right on letting him. Basil hated public shows of affection, and he and Neva had always said that sort of stuff was better done behind closed doors. Nobody needed to see you kissing someone. When the man went into the barn, the woman went to the big red truck he'd just noticed. When she took an armload of shopping bags into the barn, he went to see what else was in it.

Clothing mostly, along with some food. He took a loaf of bread from one of the bags, and a bag of lunchmeat, then found a place to hide and eat. He was just making him a sandwich when the man, bigger looking now that he was closer to him, took in more things. Basil ate three sandwiches before he made his way back to the truck.

He'd never thought about needing a gun before, not in all the years that he'd been living out here in the middle of nowhere. But the gun, just a handgun, was lying on the truck bed like it was begging him to take it. Grabbing a few more items as well as the gun, he made his way back to the woods just as the woman came out. He sat down to see what he had when she left him again.

There were apples in one of the bags. Not usually something that he ate, but he couldn't remember the last time he'd filled his belly and ate two of them as he searched the rest of the stuff. The gun was in his pants pocket for now.

He had managed to snag him another Baggie of meat...this one he thought was turkey. There was some cheese, too, but he avoided it. Cheese gave him gas, and Neva had made him promise to never eat it again. Basil thought it was a good idea, even though for now he was out of doors. There were some snack crackers that he put back in the bag, as well as a bag of something he'd never eaten before called bagels. They were bread that tasted all right, but were a little tough for him. He ate one of them as the couple moved into the barn again.

Basil had no idea what he was going to do with his bounty, but sat with it all around him. When the woman came out of the barn again and moved to where the workers were at the house, he moved along the tree line to watch her. She was sure pretty, and he thought maybe she was younger than he'd first thought. But Basil had never been good as guessing anyone's age.

Neva told him one time that he'd never make it as a barker in a circus. He'd be giving away all the profits when he had to start off as the guy who guessed your age. Even having a five-year span to get it right, he'd still get it wrong.

When she stopped moving and turned in his direction, Basil was sure she'd seen him and stilled. But she only looked around before making her way to the truck. Basil decided to ask her what she knew of Dawn and where he might find her.

But things took a bad turn when she saw him. Basil was sure she was gonna scream her head off, but she only stared at him. It wasn't until the man came out of the barn that he lunged at the girl to try and keep her from yelling her fool head off. Pulling her body in front of his, Basil reached for the gun and pressed it into her head. The man stopped, but he didn't look like he was going to stay stopped for very long.

~~~

Dawn was terrified. The man behind her had given her so much grief as a child and young woman that she wanted to scream and run. But she felt the gun bite into her head and she remained still.

"Let her go." She looked at Ellis as his wolf moved over his skin. "You either let her go or I'm going to kill you when you do."

"I need to find her. Just find her. It's all gone, all of it, and I just want to find her." She asked him who. "Dawn. I need to find her. I need…it's all gone. Everything I loved is all gone. My Neva and my house. Who takes a person's house and crunches it all up like that? Not nice people. Not nice at all."

Honey, I need you to look at me. She looked at Ellis but listened to the man holding her. *When I tell you to, I want you to just try and get away from him.*

No. Ellis, don't touch him. He looked ready to argue with her, but she cut him off. *Listen to him. Listen to what he's saying.*

"I can't even bury her. There ain't no money, and that ambulance driver, he done took it all from me. He's having a grand time while my Neva is gone. I never should have left her. It was a bad, bad thing to do. I should have stayed and let them shoot me, but I ran away like a little boy who's wet his pants. I should have stayed. I should have stayed with her."

Ellis seemed to calm then. And when the others, most of them wolves like him, came from the construction site to help, he stopped them as well. Dawn let out a slow breath, hoping what she was about to do wouldn't backfire.

"It's me, Uncle Basil. It's me, Dawn. You have me." He told her she wasn't nice, and Dawn watched Ellis as Basil waved the gun around. "Uncle Basil, it really is me. It's Dawn Whitfield. Well, it's Dawn Emerson, but I'm your niece."

"She run off. We weren't nice to her, no sir, but she had no cause to run off from us." He looked at Ellis before talking again. "That man over there, he told you to say this, didn't he? He's going to take you outta my arms and kill me. I'll welcome it, I'll tell you. I will. I could go where they've put my Neva. I'd have liked to be at the creek with her, but I just don't have no money."

"I made funeral arrangements for her this morning when we got back. I had them bury her in the cemetery out by Darcy Road. My mom is buried there, too." He told her that he wanted her by the creek. "I'm afraid we can't do that, Uncle Basil. There are laws prohibiting that."

She had no idea if that was true or not, but he seemed to consider it. "I don't have nobody left. I lost my poor Neva, and I was a bad person to leave her there to be dead all by herself."

Dawn thought about telling him that she was his niece again and his relative, but didn't. They weren't close and more than likely never would be. He was mourning the loss of his wife right now, and would more than likely revert back to the man he'd been a long time ago.

"Uncle Basil, I—"

"Stop calling me that. The brat wasn't pretty. She barely was tolerable looking, and nothing all that much of a person either. She was dropped off to us and we did our best by her only 'cause of the money. Nothing more. I hated her mother, and I didn't like her brat either. You're not her. Stop calling me your uncle."

It hurt, his words and the fact that he really believed them. Not that he said she was pretty, but the fact that he'd thought of her as nothing.

"You had a picture of your mother on the side of your bed. I broke the glass in it once and you tied me to the radiator in the kitchen for a week with nothing more than a blanket and a can to pee in. It mattered little to you that I got burned there, that the steam coming up off the thing scalded me every time it turned on. On Aunt Neva's side of the bed was a picture of you. Only it wasn't really you, was it? It was your father. You told her it was you so that you could have a picture of both your parents in your room all the time. Not just your mom." She looked at Ellis as she continued, trying to ignore the rest of the people there who were listening to her horrible childhood.

"When I was eleven, I asked you for a Christmas tree. You told me that only good children got those and that I was far from that. So the entire next year I worked on being a good girl. I never tried to run away, and I made all your favorite meals. I even lied to the teachers, telling them that you had been hurt and couldn't work, and that was why I hadn't paid my dues." She felt the tears roll down her face. "When it came time to put up the tree, to do anything related to Christmas, you remember what you did? You slapped me, knocking me against the fire grate and bloodying my head. Then you stood over me, screaming at me about how ungrateful I was. What a disappointment I had been to you, and even then you told me that when the money ran out, you'd bury me in the back yard rather than keep feeding me when I was worthless to you."

"You were forever wanting things that were stuff you didn't need. We deserved that money, not you. Putting food in your mouth was all that I could stomach when you lived with us. Then what did you do? You up and left us. Just run off like we didn't do nothing for you."

Dawn was crying, her heart broken and her mind sore from the abuse. When Uncle Basil talked about all the things he'd had to put up with, all the things he and her aunt had had to make sacrifices for to keep her in their home, she stared at Ellis, wondering what he thought of her now.

"Then you go and crunch up our home. What the heck did you go and do that for? We done never did a single thing to you to make you wanna be that mean to us." She turned then, jerking from his grip and shifting at the same time. Her wolf tossed him back on his back, and she put her mouth over his throat. Dawn might have bitten had Ellis not spoken to her.

You kill him and it will be for nothing. She growled. *He's a prick, I'll give him that. And a monster, but killing him will not make it all go away. You're bigger than him, and he's just not worth it.*

He said the same thing of me. She felt Ellis run his fingers over her fur and then down her snout. She felt tears then; her wolf was just as hurt as she was. *He should be dead.*

Yes. He more than likely should be. But he's also mentally unstable. I think perhaps he might have been all along, but the death of his wife took him over the edge. Dawn, I'll ask you to do the same thing you asked me to do. Listen to him.

"Kill me. Kill me. You should have done it a long time ago. Kill me now. Kill me, please just kill me so I can be with my Neva." He continued to repeat it over and over, begging her to kill him.

"I've called the police. That should be them now." She heard them then, the sirens screaming toward them. "You're going to have to let him go, baby. And go into the barn to shift. If you don't, then we're going to have a lot of explaining to do."

He hated me. And my mother. Ellis told her he knew and that it was his loss. *He really didn't want me. Then why didn't he just let me go into foster care? Was there that much money in keeping me?*

Ellis told her to go again, and she let go of Basil's throat. For as long as she lived, she would never call him uncle again. Nor his wife her aunt. Just as she went into the barn, she heard Ellis tell the men to keep him there as he led the police to him. She was dressed and coming out of the barn when Basil turned to her.

"You keep her away from me. She tried to kill me. I asked her for some money, and she just went and turned on me. I need to bury my Neva near the creek. Ask her how she changed into a wolf and tried to bite my head off. She was gonna murder me, she was. Just ask her." He tried to get away from the officer holding him back, but he was a good deal stronger as a shifter, too. The officer asked her if she was pressing charges.

"Yes. We'll be doing it later today. My wife is shook up right now, and I think I'd like to take care of her now." Basil was still screaming at her, but she moved to Ellis as he continued talking to the officer. "He's the man that burned our home down. I think he's been trying to find a way to get to Dawn for years."

"We've been looking for him as well. The man who called the police when Miss Rothschild died gave us a good description."

Dawn stopped him when he started to turn. "Rothschild? I thought her name was Combs, like his." He shook his head and told her they were never married so far as he knew. "That's not possible. They were married. I saw their marriage license in their bedroom."

"No, ma'am, there is no record of him getting married. Might be that they married in another state, but we don't think so. We didn't even know there was a woman out here with him until we started doing some research. Miss Rothschild was…well, we found out a great deal about her when her body was found. After doing some DNA testing, we found out that she was a little girl who had been kidnapped about forty some years ago. There wasn't much in the way of testing like there is now, but her name and information had been added to the data base recently and she popped up when we put the results in the system."

"She was mine, and my momma wouldn't let me have her. So I took'd her." They stared at Basil as he started spewing information. "I needed her. She was the nicest person in my school, and when momma said I couldn't go to school no more, I missed her. I brought her here when my momma finally died, and we lived happily ever after, just like them stories she used to read to me."

"Why weren't you allowed to go to school anymore?"

Basil screamed at her. Not a word, just a loud scream that had her backing away from him. "I did not hurt her. I never hurted her. She was just in my way. I never hurted her." Basil struggled more and then looked at her. "You look just like her now that I see you. Ugly like her. She had an ugly mouth and an ugly way about her. Momma liked her best. Always gave her whatever she wanted. But I fixed her, didn't I? I fixed her right up, and then she had to go and get herself in trouble all on her own. All on her own. All on her own."

He was singing then, laughing at the grand joke that only he understood. She looked at Ellis when Basil was being put in the back of the cruiser, and cried when she realized how horrible of a person he'd really been.

Later they discovered the stash of food he'd taken from them. She'd thought, even then, that he was near them, but never that he'd actually steal from her. But then, he'd been a thief all his life. Why should now have been any different? Basil had eaten nearly half a loaf of bread and all the lunch meat she'd been meaning to feed the workers with. As they made their way to Addie's house, she thought of all the things that were clearer to her now that she'd never noticed as a child.

"They never went anywhere. He would call up someone and have things brought out to the house. I never left either, kept a prisoner much like Neva had been, I suppose." Ellis held her while he drove into the garage. She sat there for several minutes while he said nothing. "I wonder now what my mother was going to tell me in her letters. You think she was going to tell me more than what he did today?"

"I don't know. But I'll have Shawn bring them to you when he comes here again. I think it might be more enlightening than what Basil's been saying to you." He looked at her then. "You think he murdered his mother so that he could have Neva there with him? I mean, you said they loved each other. Do you suppose it was because she'd had no choice?"

"I don't know. But I think I want to find out." Opening the door, she got out before he could come around the truck to open the door for her. "Ellis, I love you. I'm so sorry about all this. I had no idea."

"Don't worry about it, babe. I'm just glad that he's being taken care of and out of our lives." She nodded. "We will make sure that he gets the best care. Because as much as he hated you, or professed that he did, had he not taken you, I might never have met you."

She nodded and walked into the house with her hand in his. Tomorrow was going to start a new beginning for her, and she was going to do it, too. Her business was going to be a good success and they were going to help out children that might otherwise be shoved under the rug. Tomorrow, she told herself again. Tomorrow was going to be a new beginning.

CHAPTER 15

Mike walked up to the house and knocked. He was trying to convince himself this was the right thing to do, but he was a little scared. Ellis was a good man, but things could go badly when an alpha stepped down because there was someone much stronger to lead them.

Addie was the first person he saw when the butler asked him to wait. She brought him into the living room and asked him to have a seat. He said he'd rather stand, and she sat on the long couch.

"Jarrett and Ellis are out in the back. There was this problem with one of the doors to the pool house, and they're out there being manly and fixing it. Dawn had to go into town, but she's on her way back." Mike nodded. He knew she was trying to relax him. He was tense, but not really into small talk. "That would be her now."

When she came into the room, Mike had to do a double take. She'd changed since he'd seen her last. Her entire demeanor was different, healthier even. When she asked him to sit down, he did so more because it had been a command than because he wanted to get off his feet.

"Ellis said that you wanted to talk to us both." He nodded at Dawn. "I wanted to thank you for letting us use some of the pack to help with the house. It's been all right living here, but I want to go home. To my home."

"They wanted to come here. To meet him...and you." She nodded, and he felt stupid. "You do know why I'm here, don't you?"

"Yes. I guess you don't want to be alpha anymore, and you think that Ellis will do a better job." He nodded, feeling the tension roll off him a little. "Why is that? I mean, what makes you think he'd do a better job than you are? You've more experience than he does. You're older; not old, but older by a few years. And you're already the alpha here. Why Ellis? Why now?"

"He's stronger than me no matter the age. His...he's an alpha, and you're his bitch mate." Mike flushed when she grinned at him. "I'm sorry. That didn't come out right. My wife is forever telling me to think before I open my mouth."

"I think that's good advice, but I also think you're wrong. I'm no more an alpha than...well, than Addie is. Or even Jack." Mike said that Jack was scary and that most would do as she said to avoid arguing with her. "Yes, she can be a bit opinionated. I think that's why I love her so much. But you didn't answer my question. Why Ellis, and why now?"

Mike felt like he was walking into a trap and looked to Addie to help him out of it when he realized she'd left him. Mike was trying to figure out what to say to Dawn, who, for all intents and purposes, was his alpha, when Jarrett and Ellis came in. Jarrett left much like his wife had, quietly and without comment.

"I'd like to talk to you both." Dawn laughed, and he felt his temper rise a bit. But he knew to hurt her, to even make the wrong comment to her, would be his certain death. Ellis was that strong over him. "I would like to have you take over the pack. All of it. There's a little money to be had. No house unless you want mine, and a lot of the younger ones have been leaving for a few months now."

"This is not the way this is done, is it, Mike?" He shook his head at Ellis. "I heard Dawn ask you why us and why now. Tell me."

There was no compulsion there. None. Only a man asking a question that he wanted answers to. Mike almost wished that he had used his power over him. He might have felt a little better about what he had to tell him.

"I'm not cut out for it. I don't even...I didn't want it when I took it. But there was no one else to do it. The alpha that had been the leader before had robbed the pack of all its resources and then left town. They were going to turn on the humans if order wasn't brought to them." He got up to pace. As a man who thought better on his feet, he never thought to ask them if he could until he was standing. Ellis told him to go ahead. "I like being sheriff. I mean, a great deal. The pay is better and I get to spend more time with my family. I never got to do that before because I never became the alpha so much as I babysat them. And when they didn't do what needed to be done or just ignored what I needed from them, I had to do it myself. Everything became my responsibility because it was easier than fighting with them to get things done. It was all my fault how things turned out."

"It was." Mike looked at Dawn. "I know how it happens. The floor doesn't get swept right the first time, so you show them how to do it. The next time you ask them, it's worse until you just would rather do it yourself than have to deal with them whining and complaining about how hard it was, or how much work it was. But you should have made them do it over and over until it was done by them and not you."

"I was a horrible leader." Ellis stood up then and told him he wasn't a horrible leader, but one that was in over his head. "I need you to take the pack. I can't do it anymore."

"You know that it's not that easy, don't you? I can't just take it from you because you didn't want it. There will be hell to pay for both of us and your family." Mike nodded. He'd figured this would happen. He'd have to leave the pack and move away. His family would be targeted if he didn't. "There has to be first blood."

"What?" He looked at Dawn, then at Ellis again. "I don't want to fight you. I know for a fact that you'll kill me, and even if you don't, I won't be able to support my family any longer if I do something this stupid. Just let me leave the area. I'll leave now, take my family and go."

"First blood or you stay and work this out on your own. Dawn and I are just as happy to live on our land, pay our dues to you, and watch things fall apart. You either do this the way I want, the way we want, or it's all on you."

He was going to die was all Mike could think of, and that he would never see his next child take his first breath. Nodding to Ellis, Mike felt his head snap back as pain shot through his entire body. Falling back, he landed on the couch he'd been standing near and looked up at the man.

"First blood," Ellis stated.

Blood poured from his mouth and nose. Mike reached up and wiped the blood from his face and stared at it on his hand. He'd drawn first blood; Ellis had just drawn first blood. It was just too much to comprehend, and he looked at Ellis, who was nursing his hand.

"You drew my blood. You're...you're not going to kill me."

Ellis shook his head and put out his hand. It was open, not a bit of violence in the gesture or the look on his face. When he took it, Mike felt the weight of the past several days roll off him, and he returned the hug that the bigger man gave him. Sobbing now, he was so relieved, he pulled Dawn to him for a hug too. Ellis's low growl had him backing away.

"I'm sorry. So sorry. I was caught in the moment." Ellis nodded and wrapped his arms around Dawn. "You didn't...you have no idea how...I didn't die."

"No. And you won't either, not so long as I'm here." Mike nodded again, trying in vain to control his emotions. "Mike, we're going to have to get this right. I've been looking around with the help of my brother, and things are bad here. I need to take a strong stand."

"You mean with me?" Ellis nodded. "I understand. I'm going to hurt a lot more than just the punch to the face. I'm prepared to take it."

"Good." Ellis sat down with him as he and Dawn started to outline what they had seen and how they were going to try and fix it.

There was the discipline that had to be taken care of. Most of the younger wolves had no jobs and, therefore, didn't pay dues. And it wasn't like they were high or even taxing, but they spent their money on drugs, booze, and women. There was nothing left for the pack.

The drugs were another issue. Most of them, nearly three quarters of the pack, were selling them, doing them, or making them. Mike told them how he'd tried to put down the hammer since becoming sheriff, but there simply was just too much of it. Ellis told him the next time he made an arrest, he wanted to be there, too. Just him, Ellis, and the dealer. Mike almost felt sorry for the dealer.

They talked about meetings, and Mike was ashamed to admit that those, too, had stopped. No one had shown up, and there was no one there to help with food either. Dawn told him that she had that covered and that it would be a pack event from now on or else. Mike had a feeling that even though she looked like she'd blow over in a hard wind, Dawn was just as hard and vicious as her husband.

The butler came in an hour or so later. They had moved to the dining room, papers were spread out all over the large table, and there was even a huge wipe-off board that had been unearthed from somewhere, and Mike was helping Dawn add names to it. It was a pitiful sight to see so few names on the side of being compliant.

"Mistress, there is a delivery for you."

Dawn looked at Ellis. There was fear there and a little bit of sadness. But when she got up to follow the older man, Ellis told Mike it was a package from her mother.

"I thought her mom was deceased." Ellis told him she was, but there was a package to be delivered to her after her death. "That would be hard. I knew her mom. She was dealt a hard life, I think. There are some files at the station about her, too. And the family. If she ever wants to see them, just tell her to come by. I'll make them available to her."

For another three hours, they talked and planned. Mostly Ellis did the planning, but he did ask for his input on a great deal. Dawn came back to help them, but he could tell she was slightly upset. Mike was glad now that this couple had shown up to live here. Otherwise, something else might have happened to him and his family.

~~~

The box sat on the table for three days. Dawn would walk by it, sometimes even touch it, but she'd yet to open it. She wasn't ready. And she was thankful that Ellis never pressured her in any way. Addie and Jarrett had left the day before, and now it was just the two of them in the house, if you didn't count the endless supply of household help. Dawn was sitting on the deck enjoying the warm day when Ellis came out to see her.

"I've got to go over to the house, then on into town. The pack house is being cleaned out today, and I need to be there." She looked at him, dressed in a simple pair of jeans and a tee-shirt. "You should come with me. You've not seen the house in a couple of days."

"Addie just called." She looked at the cordless phone; she hated the thing, but it had become a necessity this past week. "She said to tell you that today you should be on your best guard. Do you know what that means?"

"I think so." He sat down. "She told me that I'd be challenged. I had no idea it would be this soon, but I'm guessing that's what she means."

"Will you win?" He shrugged. "I see. And as soon as I marry you, I might become a widow. I don't think I want to know what's in store for us from now on."

"Me neither. But knowing that I need to be paying more attention today makes it a good deal nicer, don't you think?" She nodded and looked out over the pool. "What's wrong, Dawn? You've been in a funk for the last couple of days. Is it the box? I can have it destroyed if you want. Or Luke or Shawn both said that they'd go through it for you to see if you might need anything from it."

"I don't think her life was all that much different than mine." He asked her how. "She was a prisoner of Basil's, I think. Some of the things he said, some of the things that she even said. Not really saying he hurt her, but she was afraid of him."

"You think he treated her the same way he did you?" She nodded. "Do you know why she went to prison? Why she left you alone for so long?"

"I think the reason she never told anyone about me was because she knew that Basil would get me. I guess she thought—and she was more than likely right—that I'd stand a better chance of surviving on my own than I would have with him. I don't think she ever knew about Neva. Maybe she did, but she never mentioned her."

"They'd been together for a long time, I guess." She nodded. "Mike said that there were reports he'd make available so you could see if you wanted. I'm not sure what they'd be other than arrest records. Or maybe complaints."

"Complaints, I think." Dawn didn't look at Ellis, but she knew that he'd stretched out his legs. His arms were lying across his lap, and his head was tilted back to have the sun settle on it. "She went to prison because she had robbed a bank. Alone. I remember thinking at the time when I'd heard it that it would have been more money for us. Something to eat on a regular basis. It never happened, of course. It should have been a simple case of her getting arrested and put in jail for a time. I know that the gun she carried wasn't loaded. Basil told me often enough how stupid she was to have done it without bullets. But the guard at the bank tried to subdue her and pulled his gun. It went off and he was dead."

She knew all this. Had known it all her life, but the pieces were falling in a different order now that she had more information. The fact was that Basil had never shut up and that the papers were spewing his words there for everyone to read.

"Cancer took her." Dawn nodded. "So, she wasn't what made you a shifter. It must have been your father. You said she never mentioned him. I don't know a lot about shifters, but can only a mate father a child with his mate?"

"Yes. In that part we're the same. Once you find your mate, you can only have a child with them." Dawn looked at him and wasn't surprised to see that she'd been right about how he was sitting. "I don't know how she survived all those years without him. I cannot even imagine being without you for more than a few hours, so I'm thinking he is more than likely dead. Love between us for me is all consuming; I would think it would have been for him as well."

He stood up then and picked her up. Dawn felt his love for her and curled into his neck to smell his scent. Ellis held her this way for a while, and she finally told him what she was going to do. It would be easier this way.

"I want to open the box by myself. I don't know what's in it. Really, I can't think what, after all these years, she'd have to say to me other than maybe the name of the man who sired me." Ellis kissed her forehead. "I know that you need to go back to see your family tomorrow. If you don't mind, I'd like to stay here."

"No. First of all, my family will kill me if I don't bring you home with me. And secondly, whatever is in the box, it affects us both. And I don't want you finding things that might hurt you and I'm too far away to hold you. We can open it tonight if you want, or never, but I don't want you to do it alone. I can't help you if you send me away."

She started to cry. Relief was profound. Dawn hadn't even known that was what she wanted him to say until he did. Wrapping her arms around him, she held him while she cried and thanked him for being there for her when she was too stupid to know she needed him.

They were getting in the big truck when his phone went off an hour later. It was Mike. There was a problem at the pack house and it was bad. Ellis looked at her after he got off the phone.

"Don't do anything stupid. Stay by my side and, please, let's try not to kill anyone." She grinned at him. "Dawn, I'm serious."

"Oh, so am I. No one is fucking with my husband without a fight. And I promise you, when this is done, you and I are going to be the last men standing." He just shook his head and climbed into his truck. "I'm thinking this will be just what I need."

There were perhaps a dozen men standing around the pack house. Most of them were younger men, and all of them should have been at work. When they got out of the truck, Ellis warned her again to behave. But she knew just what to do. Addie had given her a little advice, too.

Take on the biggest. You're stronger, meaner, and have the most to lose. If you kick his ass first, the rest of them will see you for what you really are. A woman in charge.

Ellis seemed to know that she was going to be in the middle of things and walked beside her and not in front. They were a team, but today, she had to put up a show of force. The man in charge was a punk-assed kid, and she walked right up to him and punched him in the face.

"You touch her and I will kill you." Ellis was right beside her when he spoke. The man looked like he was going to attack but stopped to look at Ellis. "Now, you'll listen, or in twenty-four hours I will have a pack here that will kill each and every one of you without a moment's hesitation."

"You'd kill this pack to let the little woman come in and take over." Ellis growled at the man, and he growled back as he continued. Doors slammed behind her, and she was suddenly afraid. If there were more of them, this could be the end of her and Ellis. "What the hell is this?"

"I told you, my help." Ellis put his hands on her shoulders as he spoke to her through their link. *Hunter and the others are here. I just heard from them when I told them what was going on. Apparently not only did Addie call you, but she called in some reinforcements as well.*

Good. Dawn felt better about what she needed to do. "What's your name, you little piece of shit? I want to know because I want to notify your next of kin when I kill you for being stupid."

Addie whispered in her mind what his name was just as he spoke. "Rocky, like my muscles. And you are nothing to me. I'm challenging your mate for this pack. I already run it anyways, and you ain't big enough to stop me."

"Well, Donnie Jackson, you think you can take me on instead? My mate, your alpha, will let you fight me if you think that you can win." He snorted, and Ellis didn't move.

"That's right, stand there and act like you have it all together. Have control. Do you? Let's give it a try, shall we?"

She turned to the man standing beside him, an equally stupid looking kid that seemed to have more pimples on his face than he did hair on his head. Dawn had never used compulsion before, never really had a need, but she pointed her finger at the boy and told him to shift.

It was painful. Anyone standing next to him could hear just how much it had hurt him to be commanded to shift. When she turned to the kid on Donnie's other side and told him to do the same, he went down on all fours screaming, his body shifting from human to a smallish wolf in seconds. When Dawn looked at him, Donnie looked at Ellis.

"She running the pack or are you?" Ellis laughed and told him they were both going to be in charge. When Donnie looked at her again, she could see the smirk on his face and wanted to smack it right off him.

But Ellis stepped in front of her. "This is mine. Shift."

The boy did so. The pain was harsher than the other two because Ellis was that much stronger. When he ordered him to shift again, then twice more, the kid just lay there as a man and didn't move. He was in pain and a great deal of it. And there was no healing from this unless his alpha allowed it. Ellis knelt down to his level and looked at him.

"I'm not going to kill you. Yet." Donnie whimpered. "You have two choices. You can behave and get your act together, or I will kill you. Do you understand me?"

"Yes."

"What did you say? I couldn't hear you."

"Yes, sir. I understand. I don't want to die. You win."

Ellis stood up, and just as he turned to Dawn, the kid leapt. Dawn let her cat take her this time, shifting almost in mid-jump toward the younger man. He was dead even before he touched either of them. Dawn stood over his body, his throat still bleeding on the cold earth, and snarled at the others. Three of them dropped to their knees. One of the wolves that she'd made shift whimpered and fell to the ground, his belly exposed to show he was giving in rather than die.

Ellis just stood there. His brothers, all of them, had shifted at some point, and their tattered clothing was all over the ground. Ellis was a lone man standing among the Emerson wolves.

"Are you hurt?" She shook her head. "I have things in the truck for you to change into. Can you...can you do that for me?"

He handed her the bag, but he didn't touch her. She was afraid she'd done something wrong. And when she returned, dressed and human, he was addressing the pack. A great many of them had joined the group while she was gone.

"Yes, my wife is a shifter. And as you can see, well able to take care of herself and me." He looked at her as if he were looking for an injury or something. Then he looked back at the crowd. "But you will know that to harm her or to cause her to bring harm to you will result in death. I will not take it lightly if she gets pissed again."

Ellis took her hand then, curled his fingers through them, and brought them to his mouth. The look he gave her, the love in his eyes, made her realize that he'd not been mad at her, but terrified for her. And she'd been the same for him.

After the others dispersed, the pack, *their* pack, moved away. She wasn't naive enough to think it was over, but this was a good start. Ellis held her in his arms until Hunter came up and patted him on the back.

"Scared the fucking shit out of me if you want to know the truth." She told him she'd never even given anything but saving Ellis any consideration. "And that's the way it should be. You did good work here today, both of you. Ellis, letting her do this.... Man, that was more powerful than anything I've ever seen. Dad would have busted a gut and then crowed about it like it had been his idea. I'm extremely proud of you both."

Dawn decided right then and there that Ellis was never going to another meeting without her. Never would she want to hear about something like what just happened from someone else.

"Come on, love. Let's go home." And they did.

CHAPTER 16

Ellis watched her take each item out of the box. There were letters, all of them addressed to Dawn. Also a few pictures of her, but none of them any newer than Dawn at about six or so. And there was a smaller box; this one she'd yet to open. When the jewelry came out, she handed it to him, and he could see that it was cheap, handmade, more than likely something that had been made in a craft class. Each one of them had her name on them and a year. Ellis would bet they were birthday gifts. Then there was the thick envelope, another item that she laid aside.

"She didn't have much." Ellis just nodded. There was next to nothing in the box that showed the life of the woman that had saved it. "The man at the prison took pictures of her cell when she died. Said that it might come in handy sometime. It's sad, really. Depressing."

"Are you going to read the letters?" She told him she would, but not today. "I think that's a good idea. You want to take this easy? Find out what you can first?"

She picked up the file and opened it. "It's a will. I guess this was how they'd known to give me these things. I wonder why they'd even think she needed one."

He took it and handed it to Luke. He'd been the only one who had stayed after the incident this morning. Luke was reading it as she moved to the small box. It was nothing more than a shoe box, he thought, that her mom had more than likely decorated, again in some class she'd taken. It was done well. There were cut outs of flowers, some crocheted ones as well. Dawn's name was across the top of it and that, too, was done in a craft style.

"Dawn, your father's name is Theodore Whitfield. And you were right, he is deceased. His death seems to have occurred about two months before you were born. And they were married. Your mom's name is Stacy Dawn Combs Whitfield." Luke kept reading to himself after that, but laughed and then looked at her. "You are your father's heir. A very wealthy heir."

"What do you mean?" Luke laughed again and turned the computer he was working with toward them. Ellis read the name again and how the man's family had been searching for Dawn for years. "He left everything to you and your mom, then her to you. I guess since there was no real paperwork as to where you were all this time, they had others looking. As to why they didn't just ask your mom, that's something we'll have to ask them when we contact them, I guess. She would have been able to tell them. All you need to do is contact the lawyer who filed this with the state and they'll take care of the rest. Congratulations."

Ellis showed his brother out an hour later. Luke was going to contact the parties involved and get back to them. He told Dawn that he'd do it without giving them her address, which she had requested him to do. When he came back, Dawn was holding the letters in her hand. There was one in her hand that she'd been reading.

"It's the last one she wrote. About a month before she died." He sat down as she continued. "She'd given up on trying to get Basil to bring me in. He had told her that I was dead and that she was undeserving of me anyway, so it was just as well. Let me read you what she said.

"'I shall never forget you. Never for all my life. Teddy and I were so much in love. And having you, it made him so happy. I wish now I had done what he asked me to do all those years ago and taken you to his family. But it's too late now.

"'Basil tells me that you're dead. I, of course, don't believe him. It would be like him in his cruelty to tell me such a lie. But a mother knows, and I know that you are suffering a great deal at his hands. Believe me when I tell you, I am so very sorry.

"'Basil is not my brother as everyone thinks, but my captor. I don't know my mother's name, nor do I think it's important after so long. I think her dead too. Not that Basil killed her, but it would not surprise me should you find out that he had. I, like other girls, was taken from my family at a young age and given to him as a playmate. But I never liked him and he hated me for that too.

"'Finding Teddy when I did was the greatest joy of my life. Finding out that we were to have you made our love all the stronger, and so much more solid feeling to me after all the turmoil I had as a child. Running from them, Basil and his mother, was not easy, but I did it and that gave me you.

"'Teddy was from an affluent family, he said. I think he said they were from upstate. I don't know. I was to meet them at one point but he disappeared — died, I know now — just before I was to go with him to tell them we were having you. His death haunts me as much as what I did to you.'"

"She loved you very much." Ellis watched her closely as she nodded. "Luke will talk to them. They might not know anything about you other than that you're their granddaughter. Not finding you has not given them a lot to go on. I don't think it will happen, but you should be prepared if they don't want to get to know you."

"I don't care if they do or not." He was glad to hear her say that. "If they do, I'll be richer for it in terms of a family I didn't know I had. But if they don't, it will be their loss. I'm just as happy to stay here with you."

She finished the letter from her mom. Stacy Whitfield had lived a hard and difficult life, made harder because of a man who had wanted someone to play with as a child. He was going to talk to Luke about that, too, see if they could find Dawn's mother's family and give them some peace as well.

"Do you suppose the house will be done soon?" He told her what Dan had told him this morning. "So in two weeks we can move into most of the house. I'm glad. And your brother Lee said he'd help me with setting up the building for production. I had no idea there was so much specialized equipment that I'd need."

"Me neither. But he's a good one to have come and help." Lee had been so surprised when she'd asked him that he'd come to Ellis later and asked if he'd made her do it. He told Lee that he hadn't even known she was thinking of asking him to help. "I'm guessing that he's coming up next week when he returns from the trip over in the plant in Europe."

Lee was setting up a large restaurant in one of the buildings that Sloan and Hunter owned. The building employed nearly six thousand people that made cheap beads for large functions. They had acquired it when the previous owners failed to make it work. Sloan was already showing a profit and the restaurant was going to make for happier workers, something the other owner had not seen fit to do.

Ellis looked over at her then. She'd grown so quiet that he thought she was crying. She'd been doing that a lot lately. But she'd fallen asleep, curled into the chair like it was the most comfortable thing in the world. Picking her up, he took her upstairs to their room and laid her down. She never stirred as he covered her up.

Ellis loved his wife. And was gladder every day that she'd come into his life.

KATHI S. BARTON

Before You Go...

Share your voice and help guide other readers to these wonderful books. Even if it's only a line or two your reviews help readers discover the author's books so they can continue creating stories that you'll love. Login to your favorite retailer and leave a review. Thank you.

Kathi Barton, author of the bestselling series Force of Nature, lives in Nashport, Ohio with her husband Paul. In addition to writing full time Kathi likes to spend time with her eight grandkids, three children and three children-in-laws. She writes to relax and have fun.

Her muse, a cross between Jimmy Stewart and Hugh Jackman brings them to life for her readers in a way that has them coming back time and again for more. Her favorite genre is paranormal romance with a great deal of spice. You can visit Kathi on line and drop her an email if you'd like. She loves hearing from her fans. aaronskiss@gmail.com.

Follow Kathi on her blog: http://kathisbartonauthor.blogspot.com/